To Margaret

MORE THAN A YEAR IN TIME

Jane Lassen

(1st edition)

MORE THAN A YEAR IN TIME

Jane Lassen

The Book Guild Ltd
Sussex, England

First published in Great Britain in 2003 by
The Book Guild Ltd
25 High Street
Lewes, East Sussex
BN7 2LU

Typesetting in Baskerville by
SetSystems Ltd, Saffron Walden, Essex

Printed in Great Britain by
Bookcraft (Bath) Ltd, Avon

A catalogue record for this book is
available from the British Library

ISBN 1 85776 701 2

Nonsuch High School,
Cheam, Surrey.

1950–1956

in appreciation.

CONTENTS

FAMILY TREE

(Section)

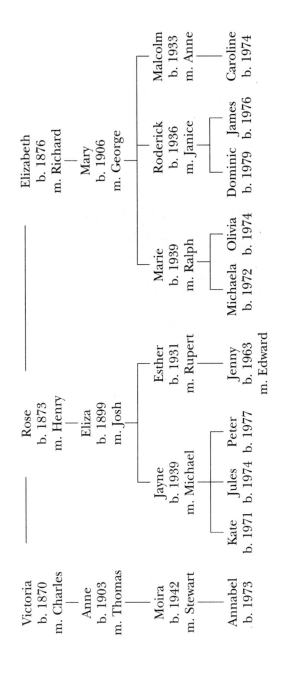

LIST OF CHARACTERS

Jayne Sanders (née Metcalf)
Michael Sanders
Kate, Jules and Peter Sanders
Inca
Rennick

Marie Travers (née Beaumont)
Michaela Kirke, Olivia Forrester

Roderick Beaumont
Malcolm Beaumont

Corina Paget
Anthony Paget

Esther Barrett
Rupert Barrett

Jenny Menzies (née Barrett)
Edward Menzies

Aunt Bethany
Mr & Mrs Stanfield
Robert and Philip Stanfield
Ella and Henry Portman

Tessa Sheridan
Will Sheridan

Vanessa Morton
Andrew Morton

Ailsa Addington
Charles Addington

1

Searching for Marie

6th July 1999

Dear Marie,

Compelling thoughts and childhood images have led me to write to you about what is happening here with the Millennium approaching and tension building up throughout the world.

Remembering and re-living our *joie de vivre* and youthful but intense interest in the countries of the world through our philately, I'm sure you share the relief I feel that the grotesquely ugly war in Kosovo is now over. This filled me with fear, with its gruesome atrocities, innocent people being shot and burnt in this day and age of civilisation. Yugoslavia has been popular with British tourists for over 30 years and we feel utter disbelief here that this is happening to these people in, allegedly, the pursuit of ethnic cleansing; but it is a comfort to know that we have organisations such as the United Nations to give protection to the victims of war.

Although we have the strength, technology and expertise in the western world to deal with these uprisings, I hope the Serbs and ethnic Albanians will learn to live together in peace. I have doubts for this generation, but optimistically, if the Germans and Jews can now tolerate one another, then the ethnic groups of the Balkans may find harmony on a different world stage.

I must confess, Marie, my thoughts are taken up with current world affairs, and you were the person, although we were children, so many years ago, that I ran to, to talk about all that was happening, for you had the same awareness.

On a lighter note, we have recently moved house and our new home has been built with the living area at a lower level than the road, looking out to a sheltered, wooded glen, which is quite enchanting. The road winds down to the lower level and I would describe the house as a designer's dream with a beautiful outlook of trees and shrubs at every angle and on different levels. The house is contemporary, warm, well-built and asking to be embellished. We are situated in a charming village with a scholarly presence of teachers, lawyers, company directors and professional people, residing with their families in a reserved and dedicated but fun-loving environment.

Michael, my husband, and I live with Julian, known as Jules, Peter and Inca the cat in this light, airy, interesting house, but our daughter Kate has had her own apartment for four years. We have developed through the passage of time into a close family. We have had some near disasters – but we have worked our way through them. The children have never given much trouble and probably the worst they can be accused of is the inevitable teenage arguing.

I thrive on the working week: the energy, output and achievement. Progress has always been more important to me than the accumulation of money, although it is all too necessary for a good standard of living, particularly, I feel, if you bring children into this world. I think of Saturday as another working day and on Sunday I relax to music and plan various trips.

Life would be unfulfilled for me without a family, and Michael, Kate, Jules, Peter and our home are the fabric of my life, but my personal interests bring colourful life to the fabric.

I do hope that this letter reaches you, Marie. Your address was given to me by our cousin Moira. It would be so interesting to take up our lives from where they abruptly separated when you were told your family were leaving the country.

Our mutual relatives have settled in different areas of the United Kingdom and we keep in touch for birthdays and Christmas, with an occasional exchange of photographs and wedding invitations.

Let me know what happened to you and tell me about life in Australia, how it developed over the years and how it differs from what you remember here.

You may ask 'Why now?'. Powerful memories are re-emerging for me as we are 'travelling' towards the year 2000, and the memory of our friendship as children has never left me.

Until I hear from you,

Sincerely,

Jayne

20th July 1999

Dear Jayne,

How amazing that you traced me to Sydney. Life seldom comes up with surprises which mean so much. I have read your letter over and over and each time, my mind travels back to different incidents at Chetworth School.

The first few years in Australia were the most challenging. I felt so different from the Australian children at that time but I was able to study art and design, eventually making it my career. From then on, I was able to take some control of my situation. Having worked for an advertising agency for five years, I decided to go freelance as an artist. Luck was on my side and one or two commissions gave me the opportunity to open my own office. I subsequently married Ralph and we had two daughters Michaela and Olivia. Ralph died suddenly with a heart attack in 1988, but it has been said that every cloud has a silver lining and my work prospered to such an extent that it has become a full-time occupation.

Time is not on my side, but please write to me whenever possible with news and views.

Your friend,

Marie

8th August 1999

Dear Marie,

With pleasure and almost disbelief, I read your letter, which took me back in time to scenes of playing fields and buttercups, hot, endless summers, printed cotton frocks and satin ribbons.

I always thought you would become an artist and I am so pleased that life has been good to you – and that you have two daughters. It must have been very difficult for you when your husband died, but your career and family obviously helped you during that phase of your life.

You have asked me to write whenever possible with news and views, as worldwide news is not always covered in the same way. I remember when we were eight years old, the way we used to search through our atlas to trace the countries of origin of postage stamps which came into our possession. On reflection, we always seemed to be talking about 'other' countries in the post-war years, from what we had heard on the radio and our parents' conversations.

4

This created a bond between us, which has survived for me in the intervening years.

Of course I will write, but perhaps I should tell you a little more about Michael and my family here.

Kate, our daughter, is 29, Jules is 26 and Peter, our younger son, is 22. We tend to be 'town' people with a love of the country and coastal areas.

When I met Michael in the sixties, he was a tall, dark, truly good-looking man, with what I would describe as masculine features. We met socially and I could tell as soon as I spoke to him that he was my 'type of person'.

We spent the evening together and he drove me home. There was a different social environment here in the sixties, with more trust in strangers and people generally. Of course, there were rogues in those days but there were certainly fewer attacks on women. The respect and the protective attitude of our fathers' generation has diminished and bullying and aggression have increased to such an extent that it is really not safe for a woman to walk anywhere here alone, day or night.

I liked Michael very much and he said he would telephone me but I did not hear until the following Thursday. I believe he was thinking this may be the beginning of a new relationship and whether this was what he really wanted at the time. He did phone and we arranged to go out together at the weekend. From then on, a day did not pass when we were not either together or talking on the telephone. We realised very quickly that we had a lot in common; he was running his own companies specialising in corporate liquidation, having qualified as a Chartered Accountant in the early sixties. I worked in London as a secretarial assistant to the Legal Director of an American conglomerate; Michael and I were very attracted to each other.

We were married three years later, following a two-year engagement, and by then we had a small home which was very special. Michael has always been self-motivated, hard-working and ambitious, with a kind, sensitive and generous nature. He is appreciative of the Church and, in conversation, he is sharply intelligent but also enquiring and more than ready to improve his knowledge of a subject or situation. This is an endearing trait. He has been very successful throughout his life, with my support, and prior to the recession in this country, we went from strength to strength from the sixties with three moves to larger houses and, of course, the arrival of Kate, Jules and Peter.

We all have our weaknesses as well as our strength, which we have learnt to live with. There have been some close disasters in business, but by keeping our nerve and being optimistic, we have surfaced and learned lessons from the experience.

Michael and I had kind, loving, supportive families. Do you remember my parents, Marie? Of course, our mothers were cousins. This closeness has continued with Kate, Jules and Peter but the young ones have a different social life to live with. They will form their own opinions based on life today, with a strong mixture of their own family upbringing and values. I am pleased that none of them have rushed into serious relationships too early. They have seen their friends' mistakes, and regular talk over dinner in the evening has sifted out some good and bad decisions.

This is how I see Kate: She is tall, attractive with fair skin and hair colouring, which is sometimes highlighted for the sophisticated lifestyle she enjoys, working with a firm of stockbrokers. As the eldest, she has always set a good example to her brothers, I am pleased to say – that is so important in a family. Kate has always lived her life according to what she knows to be right, from her schooldays. She has worked long hours to furnish her modern apartment and now that is complete, she buys very expensive clothes, which give her a successful and capable presence. She is intelligent, sensitive, nervous, organising at times, and quiet at others. Kate is a very caring person and generous at Christmas and on family birthdays; she is independent but liable to leave the room in tears if criticised and, like most people, has the occasional mood swing. Her expression tends to be more serious than smiling, which belies her inward love of life.

Kate found the courage to fly in a light aircraft in America during one of her trips, with a newly qualified pilot – just qualified on that trip – an invitation I would have turned down. She surfaced from a deep ocean dive in this country with suspected nitrogen in her blood and drove for two hours in this condition; she arrived in tears because she felt she had failed. We were all so worried that, at the first sign of pain or tingling, she would have been hospitalised. Thank God, it turned out well.

Jules is two years and ten months younger than Kate. He is fascinated with technology and has worked as a computer operator and, more recently, as a programmer, since leaving school. He is tall, well-built and good-looking. He has a happy, smiling personality most of the time. He is good fun, intelligent and musical. His appreciation of music brings his happiness to the surface and the fun in his temperament. He is the most demanding of the three young ones and prefers to go about life at his own pace. He is studious, academic and daring.

Peter is three years, ten months younger than Jules. His ambition from childhood has been to build a career in aviation but this has so far eluded him. In the interim, he is working in four-star hotels in the hope that one day he will be airborne. He has a good build, with brown hair and fair complexion. He has sideburns which give a masculinity to his appearance. He is intelligent, kind, caring, helpful, good on time-keeping and managing money. He was prone to impetuosity as a child but nowadays he keeps it under control to a large extent. One very obvious quality in his cheerful personality is that he does not allow boredom to affect him. If he is going through a quiet time or a quiet day, he will make something of it and be good company. This is fairly unusual in young people, who tend to be moody or show off if days do not go right for them.

There are signs that recovery from the recession of the 1990s is underway. People were losing their homes, businesses and jobs and most people were affected directly or indirectly through the increase in interest rates. Kate and Jules were just leaving college after years of studying and there was very little choice for them, which can seriously undermine confidence in young people. From this situation, social problems can fester, leading, in some cases, to crime and violence.

Some graduates were turning to egg packing because they were paid fractionally more than bar work. My greatest fear was for our children's lives being reduced to low standards, for which I felt personally responsible as it is my belief that I should have seen it happening. Remember the biblical seven good years were followed by seven years of famine? I would say that although one never believes this will happen, it is a good lesson to think about in life today.

Most children have infinite faith in their parents and to fail them through lack of foresight, I feel, has to be one of the worst punishments a parent can experience. However, we kept a positive attitude and a guiding light led us in the right direction. I really believe that we were given strength to deal with that phase and we have learnt from it. Once again, we feel more secure and for most people here the outlook is better.

Five years on, the characters of Kate, Jules and Peter are more defined; we still have family difficulties at times but these are usually talked through. I expect you find the same with your daughters – there is always the need to steer them, from experience, into the right direction as we see it.

I plan my day in the morning and try to make it as varied as possible – boredom causes anxiety. I divide the morning between paperwork, which covers letters which need my attention relating to the home and family and, of course, my work as an author, which is time-consuming but so important to me. I am writing a novel about people living in the 21st century, which may also serve as an informal reference for future generations. I try to allocate sufficient time for the running of the home but I must confess this becomes a little out of balance at times and more help has to be enlisted. For many years, when the children were young, I had help in the house but, however well planned, standards were never quite achieved; visitors always seemed to arrive the day before the cleaner came or I would find myself rushing around to impress the cleaner. Pristine clean makes me uncomfortable but clean and tidy is essential for me. Having said that, I am reconsidering finding more help here, on a casual basis, to spend the day in a more interesting way.

I take a complete break at lunch time for an hour or so, and after a hot facial, the afternoon becomes a 'new' part of the day. It is good to go out of the house in the afternoon, get some air, meet local people, and generally prepare for the evening at home with family and other interests.

Another hour of relaxation after dinner is reviving for us, when we catch up on news and listen to music. Any evening work is finished and then we gather round for milky drinks and any later night discussions.

There are endless discussions here, Marie, about the celebrations for the Millennium. I expect you are finding the same excitement in Australia. Kate, Jules and Peter have said they will not be going to London for the biggest firework party ever seen in this country, designed to set part of the Thames alight. In spite of the promised extravaganza,

9

the young ones have seen the difficulties and even the danger of the situation. Apart from a large dome designed to exhibit the products and aims of British companies as well as entertainment in the form of high-wire acrobatics and music, a large ferris wheel to be named the London Eye will be erected by the Thames. This will turn very slowly to give the occupants a good view of London. The dome was not very popular at the outset, but now seems to have been generally accepted. There will be parties all over the country, but a number of hotels and restaurants will not be opening on the last day of the year, due to general confusion on charges and payments to staff and, in fact, many people are understandably unwilling to work at all during this historical occasion.

There is also fear here that the country will be put into chaos at the stroke of midnight as so many of our working systems are controlled by the magical computer. Most companies have had their systems adapted for Y2K, as it is now commonly known, others will wait until the day and then deal with it but, without doubt, there will be problems for up to a month or maybe longer, according to the general feeling here at present. I feel a shiver of fear when people say 'everything' is controlled by the computer, even traffic lights.

If the onset of the Millennium is not enough to keep everybody guessing about what will happen at midnight on 31st December 1999, we also have a total eclipse of the sun on Wednesday 11th August 1999. Excitement is growing to experience this phenomenon, which has not occurred for 70 years, and thousands of people are travelling to the West Country, where the TOTAL eclipse is expected to take place, with a partial eclipse in other areas . . .

Yesterday, we experienced the eclipse.

Rennick the gardener, Michael and I were here when it occurred. St Michael's Mount, the Isles of Scilly and Penz-

10

ance on the western side of England were slowly transformed from light, sunny and warm areas into cold, dark and eerie places. It took two and a half hours for the moon to pass from the top right-hand corner across the sun, covering it in totality until the corona round the sun appeared. As the eclipse was about to begin, the temperature plummeted from being a very warm day in August, which made the change more extreme. I was pleased that someone else was here. It was comforting that Michael, Rennick and I went through this together – nothing could have come closer to the end of the world than this change. One felt that a MASSIVE FORCE OF NATURE was slowly overwhelming the universe as the solar system was changing, over which we, the mere inhabitants of the earth, had no control.

Rennick seemed completely unconcerned and went about his duties as usual.

Shortly after the moon passed over, we looked at the garden, which is partly shaded at all times. I will never forget the picture before me. Half of the garden to the left was as dark as the middle of the night and the other half was brilliant with summer sunshine – no shadows. Michael and I went into the garden and it really was very romantic standing there watching nature change with a force that a film mogul could not even dream about.

The memorable points of the total eclipse were the darkness, without normal shadows, during the August heat and sunshine, the coldness reminding us of how the earth would be without the sun, the EERINESS OF LIFE WITHOUT SUN and the wonderful splendour when the SUN EMERGED IN THE HEAVENS TO GIVE US LIGHT AND WARMTH; a truly religious experience.

Until I write again, Marie,

Jayne

Dear Marie,

It is now a week since the eclipse and we have a new moon, according to my calendar, which apparently brings changes in the weather and the hot summer has changed to heavy rain and thunder.

The difficulties in this country seem trivial compared to what is happening in America. Tornadoes have torn up complete residential areas. Disney World in Florida has been VACATED – can you believe that? What is happening to the climate, Marie? Shops were boarded up and the residents left for a safer place. A hurricane whipped around Florida, with the full impact felt in Cape Fear – appropriately named.

As if tornadoes and hurricanes are not enough, the worst earthquake for 20 years has devastated Turkey during the night. Are you getting news of this? These sudden, disastrous occurrences have been totally unexpected in residential areas where generations have lived from time immemorial. People were killed in their sleep and thousands were injured. Apparently, blocks of flats and other buildings came down, and, it is believed, 10,000 people could be buried under the rubble. This reminds me of 1943/1944 when you and I heard about our neighbours being brought out of the rubble in the bombing. We have it in our power to stop wars but not the path of nature. The inevitable shock waves followed. How can a whole nation vacate? Holiday regions which we have taken for granted for years will have to be rebuilt.

The hole in the ozone layer is believed to be causing the changes, and control of chemicals, gases, sprays and general pollution should allow it to repair itself naturally. It seems to follow that this may be the cause, or part of the cause. The Dickensian 'Christmas card' winters of the early 1900s, were certainly colder than our winters nowadays unlike yours in Australia.

It is a bonus that this has gone in our favour here. Weeks of snow lying about from December is a memory and the once obligatory coal fire has, largely, been replaced with central heating. But the ice caps are thawing. Our risk would be greater than yours with flooding – but life has never been without danger, and optimism carries us through.

A month later.

The cooling of the temperatures and the brilliance of the autumn sun today have done wonders for me. I feel my natural energy returning after being drained by the summer heat.

It is now September, the time when the Notting Hill Carnival brings colour and excitement to London, and each year it seems to grow in exuberance. Artistically, you would find it interesting. It has become more and more extravagant in design over the last 20 years. Imaginative costumes represent aspects of the Caribbean and similar areas. Elaborate sound systems are moved into the areas on the day and exotic food is produced. A wonderful party is enjoyed by most people, with the exception of a small minority of people who, inevitably, spoil the concept. Guns and knives are brought into the area and we hear of at least one fatality every year.

Our police have gone through very difficult times in the last few years over issues such as institutional racism. True, there have been unsolved murders, but the victims have been of both ethnic and white origin. I believe there will always be differences between races, but apart from the fact that we live in a small island, every country should have a quota of immigrants.

Now to family matters. Last Sunday was a cool but sunny autumn day and perfect for spending an afternoon by the

13

river. Following a build-up of pressure from work and relationships generally, I felt a few hours in the fresh air would work wonders. There is an ideal spot within one hour from home and even if it meant going alone, I had to go. I had reached a point with autumn in the air and the onset of winter approaching that I could not cook all day and listen to family situations, to be followed by another working week ahead.

Kate has been busy in her flat; Jules has recovered from over-exertion and seems to be happy working in a temporary capacity; and Peter is working at finding a new career. When this is complete, the family will be on track for more profound happiness.

Michael thought it was a good idea to drive to the river. It is either that we are very compatible in our thoughts, or he has an angelic temperament, willing to fit in with my every request. I try very hard not to take any sort of advantage of this kindness and always check that he is happy with what we are doing; perhaps that is the secret of our happiness together.

The effect of the trip was dramatic. Michael and I returned home refreshed and invigorated to take up family matters again.

Jules and Peter are both experiencing life in the workplace. I have long discussions with them about the importance of finding employment which is suitable to their character and temperament. So many hours are spent at work that it has to be right, otherwise the build-up of inward tension can eventually take weeks of recovery. Jules has youthful energy and ambition but he has had to accept how much strain he can sustain. He has been trying to work through a 20-hour day but was eventually forced to have two weeks at home through exhaustion. Obviously, strain and tension have to be thought about on a personal level. It seems to have become a way of life since the recession

14

here, with many books and publications highlighting the condition.

Millennium tension has added to the worry of the recessionary years, and road rage, shop rage and office rage are evident every day, due to the pace of life and the struggle of average people trying to succeed in a high-powered society.

Food is also a factor. Do you keep to the old-style meals we were given as children? We have found colourings in drinks have made children hyperactive. Chemicals are more available to farmers and food scares have become more common here. It seemed to begin with eggs about ten years ago, when we were told that most of Britain's eggs and chickens had salmonella. Then came mad cow's disease and CJD, the human form of the disease. Vegetarian diets then became increasingly popular and food from other countries of the world, like India, China and Italy, were welcomed as a healthy alternative. This was followed by the introduction of genetically modified food. At present no-one knows whether to accept this food or what the long-term effect might be. There are varying schools of thought on this subject and complete fields of crops have been destroyed by campaigners as no-one yet knows the value or the risks of the experiments.

I shall finish here today, Marie

Jayne

5th October 1999

Dear Marie,

Horror, disbelief, injustice and anger is spreading through local communities in and around the London area. Today, 5th October, people routinely prepared for work, trustingly boarded their trains to do a fair day's work for a fair day's pay, only to be caught up in carnage that the worst nightmare could not equal.

In the early morning rush hour there was a horrifying collision between an express train travelling into London and a commuter train outside Paddington Station. They collided with such a force that the slower train rollercoasted over the top of the express and a carriage burst into flames. One train was cut in half, coaches were welded together and there was dense smoke. People were thrown from the trains onto the track and injured people have been helping others. This is London, England, Marie, where this sort of accident does not happen – in our lives, anyway.

Public spirit is always there and, apparently, a young girl gave her coat to a dying person. She left her name in her coat, and she was presumed dead for several hours until she realised what had happened and phoned her family and friends. Other people were lending their mobile phones to dazed passengers struggling to realise what was happening. Others were muttering that this was the second serious accident on this track in two years. The emergency services were excellent; a fleet of ambulances, medical teams and firemen arrived to give help and comfort to the victims. Forty people have been killed and a further hundred were injured. It seems the cause of the disaster was either signal failure, human error or damage to the track.

With the approach of Millennium night, and the subject of trains and who will drive them on that evening, with staff not wanting to work and volunteers being recruited with huge amounts of money being waved in front of them, this may be a strike of lightning to warn all concerned of the risks.

Speaking of risks, it is now two years since Princess Diana was killed in a car accident in Paris. You may read that the

16

truth will probably never be known. It was a terrible incident.

In my opinion, Prince Charles is a very good father to his sons Prince William and Prince Harry, and it will be interesting to see whether he will marry again. There are many issues to be resolved as he is the future King of England and Head of the Church of England.

Have you been following the uprising in Timor? I turned to the atlas and found that this is, in fact, in your geographical region of the world, so perhaps you have more detail than I have here about the rioting which has broken out over Independence in Indonesia. Apparently, the worst problems are in East Timor, where their army has killed and evacuated the troublemakers to restore peace and normality to the region. I have heard that the leaders in this part of the world are ruthless disciplinarians and if the people rebel, it is swiftly dealt with and in this way they live in peace on the whole.

The United Nations have arrived in the area but the Indonesian Government prefer to deal with matters themselves. I think, with communications and travel being so advanced, we probably tend to overlook the differences in culture and possibly fail to respect their attitudes.

Our news is that over a thousand Timorese have taken refuge in Dili to escape the militia and the United Nations had to delay leaving the area. The country is now virtually out of control and, where possible, the people are escaping to West Timor.

A British warship will go to the South China seas, but I do hope that this country will not be drawn into war with other countries. America will not send peace-keeping troops but President Habibe of Indonesia has asked for more emergency 'back-up' for this region.

We are committed to humanitarian causes here and there is provision for a massive defence budget but I believe there has to be a balance between the needs of the country and those overseas.

How would you select which cause to support, Marie? Let me know what you think – and I would be pleased to hear about the views on the Indonesian situation in your part of the world.

This time of the year always reminds me of the long summer holidays when the children were young, the fears of letting them go out to play with their friends, being careful not to 'smother' them and yet at the same time concerned all the time they were out, that accidents would happen and, in fact, should they be allowed out at all without an adult? I had to rely, largely, on their common sense and, of course, Kate was very caring and sensible with her young brothers.

When the children returned to school, my weight of responsibility was lifted and their education re-started; holiday learning was never a great success as the atmosphere was lost and there was an element of frustration for me in trying to do two jobs. So, in many ways, the beginning of the autumn term was a time to relax a little and think about plans for the future. Coincidentally, the political parties publicly discuss their plans for the future and every year I listen with interest to their manifestos.

This year the New Labour party is looking for modernisation and getting away from Conservatism, which, they believe, tried to prevent some of the country's greatest ideas such as votes for women and the formation of the National Health Service. Those are two issues which have dramatically changed our lives, as you know.

Fox-hunting is another contentious issue. New Labour believes that the thousands of supporters of the Countryside Alliance, who are in favour of the hunt, represent people who are holding back the country. They want equality of opportunity for all and for everyone's worth to be recognised. I am wondering if losing our old traditions will seem so good in the future. The party believes there is more to do to satisfy the Labour voters, such as overcoming child poverty and helping poor pensioners, but they believe the foundations of a new Britain have been laid.

There are changes in store for us, Marie, such as 'top jobs' will be given to women and black and Asian people; there will be more money for the National Health Service, with priority for cancer and cataracts, dentistry and drug-related care. A new system to catch criminals through DNA databases is being developed and the Labour party is looking for a better moral purpose and life for children and their education.

I agree that all people should be given equal opportunities, providing all people work for these better standards.

Since the recession, inflation has remained low, which, in keeping down interest rates, has encouraged industry and the country in general. A decision will be made on changing to the euro when the economic conditions are right.

I would be glad to hear of any political changes in Australia, quite apart from a percentage of the people wanting the country to become a republic.

Until I write again,

Yours

Jayne

11th October 1999

Hello Marie,

Today's news is that Michael has asked me to work for him, just for a day to catch up on some work. I will in an emergency but I am deeply engrossed in writing my book.

When the children finished their education I graduated as a designer of interiors to satisfy a creative urge after the emergence of technology. Suddenly, there seemed to be a sea of computers and artificial light; the beauty of nature was taking second place. Nature is our bible in design from where we derive most of our inspiration and it was important at the time, but somewhere along the route I decided that I would not make a commercial business from it. I delved into the past and remembered the complete satisfaction of working on an executive level for a huge American company in the West End and had visions of running a successful secretarial agency; we have to try these ideas but the end result, unfortunately, was that on completion of the work, the people who came my way were pleased with the work but had a phobia about parting with money. The ever-changing scene in computer technology also put the dampers on the idea. It was a turbulent time, but I am now channelling my energy into compiling a book and this is my 'calling'.

Now to other matters. Thousands of people will have to be conveyed to and from their destinations in London on New Year's Eve – a formidable thought that London could be brought to a virtual standstill – but how will train drivers be persuaded to work on that night?

Jules and Peter looked up when they heard the rail companies are offering £1,000 per shift and this is also available to volunteers ... I will not think about what may happen if volunteers are attracted to the money, so soon after the Paddington crash. Hopefully, there will be some criteria involved in the selection of manpower.

The roads here are also a huge problem, unlike your vast stretches of open roads and outback. The public, in general, are dissatisfied with trains due to lateness, increased fares and accidents. Petrol is going up in price for whatever reason and although people always find money for petrol, I sense the companies cannot afford the high prices. We have a new written test and photo-licences here now for drivers but in spite of all measures, it appears the roads are getting closer to gridlock every day.

There have been problems at this late stage with the London Eye. This is similar to a giant funfair Ferris wheel. The construction company have been unable to raise the wheel from the ground; several cables snapped. Jules will go on every ride in a theme park and the idea of those cables and brackets snapping on a wheel which is 450 feet in the air cannot be contemplated. Having said that, it is a huge project with deadlines. Electricians are also striking for better pay and conditions – I believe they probably have a good cause.

We have always been survivors, Marie, so we shall see.

Yours

Jayne

15th October 1999

Dear Jayne,

I was so pleased to read your last letter. We had many interests in common and I am delighted that you graduated in interior design; how I would love to see some of your work. Your sons have a good sense of humour if they are willing to drive trains for the first time, for £1,000 per shift. How are your nerves with Jules riding high in the theme parks? Seriously, my nerves were shattered after the voyage in 1947, followed by being home-sick to an extent I can hardly describe. Eventually, as I was young enough I was able to block out the trauma, but I will never forget England and our infant years together. What was your earliest memory?

My view on Timor is that they have a good regime but it would be difficult to adopt in the western world. As far as Government spending is concerned, budgets should be adjusted, annually, to help overseas countries, giving donations according to priorities.

I will have to finish here due to pressure of work, but please don't forget me, will you?

Your dear friend Marie.

24th October 1999

Dear Marie,

Your letter arrived two days ago, but due to a backlog of work, I have only just been able to turn to the computer and write.

It must have been a great adventure for you when you first arrived in Australia with your family. I am sorry to hear the voyage made you ill, particularly as you were at sea for so many weeks and that you felt homesick for England and your friends all those years ago. Although you only had your family in Australia to communicate with about your life in England up to eight years of age, but you clearly grew into the Australian way of life with new friends. As you say, part of you will always be English. I will never forget the years at Chetworth School, either, and also have colourful memories of the children, the staff and everything that happened during those few, early years. I still have the stamp album you gave me and I frequently turn the pages.

Michaela and Olivia are lovely girls; thank you for the photos.

It is good to hear your opinion on Timor and your priorities on Government spending if you were running either the UK or Australia. As life and the world are always changing, I agree with you that budgets probably need to be adjusted on an annual basis, but it does seem sensible to remember that 'charity begins at home' and the needs of one's own country should be met before other humanitarian causes. It should follow that the strong nations can then help the weak.

You asked for my earliest memory, Marie. Having thought hard about that, I think I have to say it was my Aunt Bethany's wedding and, about that time, I have early memories of staying with my paternal grandmother in the forties.

Briefly, I remember the layout of my grandmother's bedroom, where we were shown, to be dressed for the wedding. I wore a long pink dress to my ankles, a pink bonnet from which I could just see out from underneath and, best of all, a pink muff, of which I was very proud. The wedding and everything that followed is a complete blank – I obviously had a passion for clothes in those days as that is all I can remember.

The visits to my grandmother mainly included putting jig-saws together, consuming my favourite fried tomatoes by a large coal fire and cooker combined and playing with other children in the neighbourhood. I usually stayed for three months at a time and also felt homesick so I appreciate what the early days were like for you so far away from home.

I cannot tell you how pleased I am that we have made contact again through correspondence. We were always so full of bubbling information and chatter and also so receptive to one another's news of the day. It would have been such a waste of a good friendship if we had been separated for life. Let us try to bridge the gap of the lost years and soften the harshness of being wrenched apart without anyone listening to how we felt; but how could they?

Until I write again,

Yours,

Jayne

27th October 1999

Dear Marie,

There is dedicated planning at present to stock up one's cupboards with as much food, drink and other commodities which may be needed for up to one month after the Millennium. Stories are rife that banks will be disrupted, people will not have access to their money; adequate amounts of money should be drawn out before the end of the year. The banks are allowing £50 BILLION to cover the New Year period. I shall probably keep a month's supply of frozen food and tinned food in the house, with sufficient money in order to keep away from the banks. Even if it is all 'hype', it would be silly not to heed the warning.

An interesting subject has come up this week which illustrates the changing times in which we are living.

To begin, I recently saw a film with Kate on Oscar Wilde, the brilliant Victorian writer. When his lifestyle was revealed, he was sent to a hard labour camp by the courts in punishment for being homosexual. Life in the labour camp, working a treadmill, nearly killed him and he never fully recovered.

This year it has been agreed in America that two male homosexuals have the right to be named as the legal parents of surrogate twin babies, making legal history. It is the ninth case in America, but their application was refused here in England four years ago. Apparently, the birth certificate will show both names as parents, the non-biological father as well as the biological.

Here in Britain, the surrogacy laws still prohibit unmarried couples from becoming parents of a surrogate baby. I, personally, believe that in all cases affecting children, the child should be considered first and I feel it is just a little too early for a growing child to feel happy and comfortable with two male parents when most children have a mother. It is important for everyone to recognise themselves as they are but, in my opinion, a little girl needs a mother with whom to identify. Time will tell as to how this subject develops.

Are you interested in Formula 1 motor racing, Marie? It is one of our family leisure pursuits. Personalities and glamour have become larger than life in recent years. You have probably heard of the commentator Murray Walker, who shows such excitement during the races that he gives the coverage a third dimension. He is knowledgeable, informative and he has such enthusiasm that you cannot pass the television without looking in. I have to stop, look and listen when his strong, high-pitched tones soar above the power of the engines.

The final two races of this season were held at Sepang, Malaysia, and Japan. The Grand Prix has never been held in Malaysia before this year and a brand new stadium has been constructed for the event. In keeping with motor racing, this race was as unpredictable as ever.

I think this is an interesting situation. The outcome was that Eddie Irvine and Michael Schumacher, both driving for the Ferrari team, were awarded 1st and 2nd places. This was later annulled owing to the fact that the bodywork of the cars was slightly shorter than required by the technical regulations, which, it is claimed, gave Ferrari an advantage over the other teams. Mika Hakkinen, in third place, was declared the winner, whilst waiting for the outcome of an appeal at an international court. However, Ferrari's appeal was successful against their disqualification at Sepang.

Let me know if you are interested in the sport, otherwise, I may be tempted to go into the subject at length. The final race in Japan was won by Eddie Irvine, but the overall driver's championship was awarded to Mika Hakkinen for past successes throughout the season. We are told that although faster cars are being built, safety for the drivers is improving and really television entertainment, quite apart from actually visiting Silverstone here, would not be the same without motor-racing, for me at any rate.

Ironically, a builder's truck has just skidded while going too fast, at the end of the garden. The driver has tried to correct it and spun off the road, through two heavy iron gates and finished up 100 metres into a paddock with horses. The driver was not hurt, but shaken and he is now waiting for the recovery vehicle to pick him up. A number of drivers have approached the bend too fast and have been unable to control events.

There is also great excitement here about the London Eye, the giant Ferris wheel, which is now in place beside the Thames. In the lifting operation, cable brackets snapped, as I told you in my last letter, and it had to be delayed for a month. In the second attempt, it took three hours to raise the wheel THREE degrees. It was then lifted to EIGHT degrees. Then the cables, cranes and humans needed a rest. It was planned to reach SIXTY-FIVE degrees in the next lift and eventually the wheel was upright on 17th October 1999.

In two weeks' time, 32 viewing capsules each designed to

26

hold 25 people will be fitted to the wheel. The first passengers will be allowed on the wheel in January 2000, but it will be open for the Millennium. To show the magnitude of the project, the wheel weighs 1,600 tons and will stand 450 feet high. Originally the wheel was to be moved after the celebrations but there is now a possibility that it may become a permanent landmark in the same way that the Eiffel Tower, which was erected for the Paris Exhibition, was allowed to remain . . .

Just ten days have gone by and the wheel has been invaded by a group of Spanish people, who climbed to the TOP with a banner and a hammock, food and water to demonstrate against dams being built in Spain!! There was a Force 8 gale, which is not unusual in the run-up to Halloween, and all but one was forced to come down. The last protestor followed in his own time and we are told security will be strengthened round the wheel.

There is so much rebellion in the world at the moment and yet today, 27th October 1999, we have a beautiful cool, dry and sunny autumn day with varying shades of yellow, gold, rust and brown creating a perfect landscape – how can these people throw all this away through fighting and bloodshed?

This makes me think of Ireland and the Good Friday agreement, which took days and nights to put together by the Government and all concerned to change the course of history and put an end to misery for the Irish people . . . but it has not been signed because, broadly the IRA will not hand in their weapons. For hundreds of years there has been conflict between Protestants and Catholics leading to sectarian murders and it seems to me that it is unlikely to be resolved, owing to a complete lack of trust on all sides. The casualties of this conflict are too numerous to mention but changes are taking place.

We have just heard that the police force there, known as

the Royal Ulster Constabulary or RUC, is going to be renamed 'The Northern Ireland Police Service'. There will be more Catholic recruits in the force, committed to human rights and there will be a board of 19 members to whom the Chief Constable will report. Small groups are ever present, but there seems to be some progress, albeit slow.

28th October 1999

The following day

Pre-Millennium tension is still growing but everyone is stoically doing their duty for the effort and we have today heard the manifesto for the Conservative party, which follows the Labour plans, as day follows night.

Europe seems to be the centre of attention, as they want freedom to decide whether to carry out laws beyond those of the single market. Otherwise, we shall all become part of a 'federal' Europe and the 'flexibility' clause will be the only get-out to keep our sovereignty here in the UK. Decisions have not yet been taken on the euro currency but it somehow seems inevitable as we are now part of the EU.

Your friend

Jayne

7th November 1999

Dear Marie

Everywhere I look now there are carpets of discarded leaves. Booted people with rakes are making some impression on clearing the debris. Palls of smoke drift into the roof line; there is a dank smell of autumn in the air with shafts of late summer sunshine penetrating the darkening skies, and we have all had a bad experience centred round Jules.

We received an invitation, as a family, to fireworks at a large country house, set in five acres of ground, making a perfect backdrop for an outdoor party. Jules has known the family for 12 years and worked for them for a year or two with their sons Marcus and Dominic, keeping the office records of the family computer business, answering the telephone and meeting clients. It seemed to be the perfect arrangement as Jules had just left school and the family were pleased to have a friend in their midst. They were very kind and generous and their sincerity to Jules is unrivalled.

Kate had taken a week's holiday from work and liked the idea of rounding it off with a party, so we agreed to go, except for Peter, who keeps well away from fireworks, which we can only surmise is attributable to a childhood experience of which we are unaware.

The party began at six o'clock for the children of local friends. There was great excitement, with the little ones running in and out of the garden, laughing and jumping in anticipation. The display was on time and by 7 o'clock the adults happily streamed into the house with their glasses of wine to recover some warmth.

We were in the kitchen, which has a lovely old pastoral setting, newly refurbished with dried flowers and herbs adorning every corner and ceiling, when suddenly the phone rang. Corina, the mother, picked it up, said a few words, turned to me and said, 'It's Jules, he's been involved in an accident on the M23.' In that split second, the word 'accident' numbed me through, particularly as she had said 'motorway' . . . but Jules was speaking, although faintly, on the phone and my next thought was, 'He must be all right – stay positive.' Jules was barely able to explain where he was on the M23 and there was no time to be wasted with unnecessary conversation – it was more important to get on with what had to be done. He said he was shaken but all right and I reassured him that we would leave straight away and should be with him within the hour.

I explained to Corina, who looked startled, knowing how much the family like Jules, that unfortunately we would have to leave the party straight away. She quite understood and hoped that I was all right. I gathered up Michael, who was enjoying himself drinking wine on the patio with some friends and said, 'Jules has had an accident and I will explain on the way.'

At this point, I am not sure what gives one that inner strength to deal with what has to be done. I am naturally of a sensitive disposition, like most people, and I have to say to myself that this is life on earth and at times we have to take what comes, however harshly dealt it may seem. I clung on to the fact that I had spoken to Jules.

We had a long drive from the party to the M23, during which time I drove like an automaton with feelings numbed but senses working. For what seemed like the whole journey, Michael, who was the passenger this time, so that he could have a drink and not drive, kept saying, 'If Jules approached the M23 from a different direction, we are going entirely the wrong way.' I agree there was a slim possibility this could have happened and, if so, we would be driving for two or two and half hours retracing our route, not one hour as expected.

Jules had phoned on the mobile phone belonging to the person with whom he had the accident, an off-duty policeman, so there was no way we could contact him. In some ways, I thought I should have checked these details; on the other hand, instinct plays a large role. It was more than 95% certain that he did approach the motorway from the usual route, but uncertainty added to the worry while driving.

I have thanked God on many occasions and this was one

of them – when we reached the M23 to see Jules parked on the hard shoulder, patiently sitting there, on what I can only describe as a race track. He was cold and shaken; the offside wing was a cavity but it could have been the whole front of the car with the sort of impact which was caused through the bunching up of vehicles travelling too fast and close. It could have taken his life. The police were very busy with firework night and there wasn't a policeman in sight, although the other driver had reported the accident.

We all arrived home one hour later, tired but relieved. Peter was pale with worry at home because Kate had phoned him and said, 'Jules was in shock through a car accident.' I explained that I hadn't been able to get to a phone. Jules' car was written off but we are still a family and I shall probably think of that night whenever we celebrate the Fifth of November.

I hope all is well with you.

Yours,

Jayne

2

The End of an Era

14th November 1999

Dear Marie,

It is a beautiful sunny day with a clear blue sky; the trees are nearly bare but the leaves are still fluttering down in character with late autumn. The garden is untidy; nature never fails to deliver.

The summer flowers have been moved and winter plants are in place to brighten the cold, frosty days that come with the onset of mid-winter and I feel the beginning of the bustle towards this very special Christmas and Millennium. One has to allow for panic which will inevitably set in; this, coupled with black ice and frost, will cause more chaos and the Millennium celebrations, I fear, will give good reason for people to go 'over the top'. How is it all progressing in Sydney, Marie?

My own preference is to 'opt out' of this sort of revelry, which so often leads to tears. We have one life and I believe it should be respected and treasured. The magnitude of the occasion, as we move from 1999 to 2000 can be experienced with just as much depth of feeling, surely, without courting trouble or even disaster.

There are five full weeks to prepare for the festive days ahead and I am sure most people will enjoy themselves. Christmas, the winter solstice and the Nativity give warmth

32

to this bleak time of the year. Many issues will be put on hold until the New Year, such as the ongoing farmers' dispute with France over our beef exports and BSE in cattle but, in the meantime, many farmers in this country are slaughtering herds of cattle, losing their businesses and looking for other ways of making a living.

There are several discussions in progress here, such as whether fox-hunting will be abolished, the election of a Mayor for London and peace in Ireland, which we hope is closer than ever.

The situation in Ireland is like a small volcano which continually smoulders, occasionally erupts but, I fear, will always be there.

Speaking of smoke, haze and sulphur smells in the air, yet another change is taking place, Marie. Where Guy Fawkes failed in his plot to blow up Parliament and the firework was created, the Government are now 'phasing out' the House of Lords. Only 75 peers have been allowed to stay for this stage. There will be a second stage but this may take a lifetime. The Peers are descendants of famous and infamous people and it seems that many of those who were voted out wished to stay, as it has become an important part of their lives in advancing years, and many who were voted in would have been quite happy to give it up. I wonder if all this turmoil and so many changes at once are right for this country.

Having said that, all in the same week, I believe you in Australia have been voting on whether the Queen should continue as Head of State or whether to elect to become a Republic with a President. The figures I have are that 55% voted to keep the Monarchy and 45% of Australians want a Republic. I read that a President elected by the people was not 'on offer' and the Republican leader thought this was responsible for losing the vote. I would imagine you would prefer to have the Queen and Monarchy, Marie – am I

33

right? I also read that the Australian people voted for the Monarchy as it was better than going into the 'unknown' but I feel this is somewhat unsupportive of the work our royal family have done for the Commonwealth. Let me know, Marie.

Yours,

Jayne

26th November 1999

Dear Marie,

The '9 a.m. to 5.30 p.m.' England you left has become a 24-hour society but the holidays are longer so we shall work very hard until Christmas Eve and then it will be quiet until the dawning of the new era . . .

In this last week in November, surprisingly, people in general are not making bookings for Millennium night. There has been such anticipation and planning by promoters but they are now auctioning tickets and losing money – this illustrates the unpredictability of human nature and, of course, it is also related to money matters. The prices being quoted for Millennium entertainment have at least doubled here as the organisers will have had difficulties finding staff to work at all and those that will work will probably want double time in wages. Some venues have taken the decision to close for the night.

Threats of bombing have been made by the IRA, and with the side of human nature which likes to 'live on the edge', realistically there will probably be casualties from the celebrations as well as uprisings in parts of the world and fighting for democracy as if there is no tomorrow.

In the years we have been apart, one would expect

34

progress and even more sophistication in the world but, from the days we collected stamps from most countries, there have been wars in Iraq with Saddam Hussein attacking Kuwait and the oil refineries, ethnic cleansing in Yugoslavia and fighting for independence in Indonesia. Chechnia has broken away from Russian communist rule, the Pakistan military have over-run the Government to end corruption and Pakistan and India now have nuclear weapons. We are privileged that we have secure lives in our own countries.

As the year is closing, there are still more ideas for significant changes to be made. The latest shake-up to our long-standing tradition is the suggestion that our Monarch could be Roman Catholic and that the Monarch could marry a Roman Catholic, in future years. The religion of this country was 'set in stone' centuries ago, and the Act of Settlement of 1701 prohibits a Roman Catholic from succeeding to the throne or marrying into the religion. A Bill will be introduced to Parliament to give equal rights of succession to Catholics and the Ministers are expected to give their support to the Bill. As the Prime Minister is against discrimination, it would appear that these proposed changes represent his vision for the new century.

Our parents' era believed it was wrong for people of mixed religions to marry but Michael and I believed it was wrong for religion to create barriers and be the cause of hatred and fighting; surely, love and a peaceful existence should be the basis of religion. As you know, Marie, we went to a Church of England school and I was brought up in that belief; Michael is Roman Catholic and the children have the choice when they are ready to make a decision. My belief is that religion is the worship of God, our creator, and living one's life with respect and understanding towards each other.

It would be impossible to hold a referendum on all subjects and we will have to accept most of the changes which are planned for the new century. It would be ideal to be part of Europe without giving up our historical trappings, but I think a lot of our traditions will be confined to the history books. Our royal family have been exemplary role models and I wonder if that strength and the morale of the country will be lost in the European concept. We must be optimistic.

Yours,

Jayne

Evening – 7 p.m. 31st December 1999

Dear Marie,

It is 31st December 1999, a Friday, New Year's Eve, the eve of the new decade, a new century and a new Millennium. It is also Peter's 22nd birthday.

The excitement of this day has been slightly dulled for me as we have just had Christmas, which was a celebration and a break from the working week, but today should be unprecedented – the passing into the year 2000 is a new experience for everyone on earth but it has been, strangely, played down by a number of people, partly through an inability to cope for various reasons such as financial and also the fear of the unknown. Peter's birthday is always a positive event and everything was ready – his presents were wrapped and the cake was decorated. Kate arrived in the afternoon and the family choir sang Happy Birthday whilst he put the candles to rest. He liked our presents: a mobile phone, a motor-cycle helmet, gloves and money, and then we all parted to have a rest before the big night. TV coverage of the world began in the morning.

We had been invited to a party given by our close friends Corina and Anthony, who gave the Guy Fawkes party too, and they thought we would like to be together on this special night. We left in good time, the roads and nearby areas were quiet, but one never knows what is going on behind the scenes. At about 8 p.m. we knocked on the door and were surprised to see Corina; a guest with a drink normally opens the door and sometime later we usually find Corina lost in the crowd. However, this was different. She said, 'Where is Peter?' Peter stayed at home because he has never liked fireworks. I was, for a second, lost for words as she hasn't asked for Peter before. I fumbled through by saying, 'He is very tired,' which was true, but she was not convinced and said, 'Best to say nothing,' with her eyes fixed on me in the absence of a very good excuse. I thought that what I had said was inadequate but I now had to let it go, sensing that all was not well this evening.

Corina was dressed in a lovely black cocktail dress with a feathered hair decoration, firmly fixed, and whenever she moved her head or spoke, it elegantly waved about. She showed us into the large party room and there were about ten people huddled in one corner in dinner jackets and evening dress. As we came through the doorway, all faces and eyes turned to us. At first I was conscious that we were not in evening dress, but we had not been told and, at least, we all looked very smart. Then, of course, I realised that there was something wrong. A voice could be heard in the room saying that scores of guests had gradually dropped out throughout the day and they would be lucky to finish with 20 people. This was Millennium night; the guests who were there may have refused other invitations – and taken the trouble to organise dinner jackets and evening wear in this casual society today. They had probably gone to lengths to find babysitters, at huge cost. In spite of all this uncertainty and last-minute changes, I still prefer house parties to commercial venues which, from many years' experience, I find tend to run on oiled wheels.

Anthony came into the room in a spotless dinner jacket but his face looked very flushed against his silver hair. This was probably overexertion or anger. I gathered from what he was saying that it was anger that so many guests had cancelled their invitation at the last minute. However, Corina was undaunted and, her hair creation waving, with two or three helpers she brought in enough food, hot and cold, to feed a hundred people. Anthony put on a colourful firework display and I must say everyone relaxed and seemed to enjoy themselves. The midnight chimes were missed by whoever was in charge, on the most important New Year's Eve of our lives, and a guest decided he had waited long enough for the old tradition of Auld Lang Syne; he gathered up as many people as he could to join in the familiar dance in one large circle, and stampeded his way through it.

We all enjoyed the evening and this, as far as I am concerned, was all part of the fun.

We left about 12.30 a.m. For 45 minutes we expected to see street parties, which had been considered and talked about, although it was midwinter; there were no parties outdoor or indoor. It seemed uncanny and deserted. There were no signs of people celebrating anywhere – no music in the air, none of the usual atmosphere of this time of the year. We kept saying, 'This is very strange.' Patrolling police cars were nowhere to be seen and local rejoicing did not happen here, Marie. Following a neurotic, bordering on manic, build-up to the Millennium, a perverse and cautious quietness prevailed for us.

However, in many parts of the world, it was a day to

remember. Approximately three million people went to London, which is, apparently, a low figure. The Queen lit a beacon with a remote-controlled fuse and a million-pound firework display lit up the Thames. As predicted, there was a tremendous party but not to the extent originally expected throughout 1999. Thankfully, it was fairly peaceful with about a hundred arrests; a man fell into the Thames and died from the cold and another had a heart attack. Visitors to the Millennium Dome had a long wait to get into it and it was a great disappointment that the London Eye did not pass its safety test to take passengers. It turned with difficulty and no-one was allowed to view London from the wheel but it was illuminated with fireworks. I felt a sense of failure on behalf of the country over the safety of the wheel but it was a huge project.

We had an hourly countdown on television to midnight which continued for several hours on New Year's Day. Sunday and Bank Holiday Monday followed and today, the first working day since Christmas, it is mild with brilliant sunshine. We have had more winter sunshine this year, which helps along the short, cold, cloudy days.

I thought your display in Sydney was spectacular, Marie, and in my opinion, the best in the world. Did you go to the display or watch it on TV?

It is easy to say now, on reflection, that everyone, particularly the hospitality industry, overreacted to the new Millennium. Most people enjoyed themselves, perhaps a little more than usual overall on New Year's Eve, but it became quite obvious that no-one was willing to pay the extortionate prices which were being quoted and house parties were the favourite choice.

The so-called 'Millennium bug' has not yet materialised. It seems that the computer boffins exaggerated the difficulties which would be experienced in the change over to 2000 and many companies are now calling for an explanation as to why they spent large amounts of money adjusting their equipment . . . Such is life.

Yours,

Jayne

10th January 2000

Dear Jayne,

I am finding your letters so riveting. What fun and talks we would have if there were not so many miles between us. Jules' accident must have been desperate for you at the time – thank God he survived.

You can be sure I voted for our Queen. I am a staunch royalist and I will never change. In my opinion, this country would lose it ties with Great Britain forever, if we ever become a Republic and it might hasten my return to England. Again, we have a lot in common.

How disappointing that New Year's Eve was a damp squib for you. It is ironic how this can happen. As you will have seen on the television, the displays were awe-inspiring here, but I actually went out to dinner with some friends on Millennium night, having seen my girls in the daytime.

Take care, Jayne.

Your dear friend Marie.

15th January 2000

Dear Marie,

Thank you very much for your letter and the interesting Christmas card which you designed for the Millennium. You captured the atmosphere of your very warm climate at

Christmas, the Aboriginal history of Australia and the optimism for the future of the country. The colours of burnt orange, gold, yellow and touches of green and blue are magnificent – how I admire your talent.

I can imagine the organisation which went into the Sydney display but you are living in a very forward-thinking country which seems to have so much scope in terms of space to be developed and the exceptional climate. But how are you yourself, Marie? You say that every week you look for my letters and you feel a yearning for England which will never be there for Australia. Those first eight years were so formative; it is astonishing to realise how the programming of a child's mind begins at birth. How lovely it would be if we could go back in time and relive those early years when we used to meet at the school gate – the innocent, almost disbelief that we had been given this wonderful gift of life and how much there was to learn and enjoy with our lives before us, which at that time seemed to be forever, but on reflection it can, sadly, be a short experience.

Kate and I went to London to see the National Ballet Company perform Tschaikovsky's *Nutcracker Suite*. I felt apprehensive and slightly concerned that my nervous tension would build up in London. It must be the pace of life today, but when the nerves start to jump, there is only one cure – apart from medication – that is rest and relaxation, which is a little difficult in the middle of the West End of London. However, I believe that if we give in to this, we would never leave the front door of the house and this can cause a secondary anxiety. So I have a remedy which seems to work. Relax as much as possible on the day of the event, allow plenty of time and stay positive in the thoughts, and I must say, all the tension, apprehension and suspense seem to occur before the event and when it arrives, I usually feel much more relaxed and on top of the situation.

The evening in London made me feel years younger and

I realised that most situations can be dealt with by 'mind over matter'. The ballet was enchanting, engaging and beautiful. This sort of entertainment puts something into one's life which everyday work and worries take out. An evening at the theatre is a tonic to me, with which parties and dinner parties can never compare. This is probably because, in a way, one is still coping with people and problems; although our friends are equally important to us, there is, no doubt, more participation and effort involved.

Kate seems to be making plans and enjoying herself before she settles down in life, and the boys coped well in my absence, which was encouraging.

The Christmas decorations will now be confined to the attic for another year and it always seems to be a good time to start the spring cleaning. The days are getting longer; the weather is bright, clear and sunny, and the moment seems right to put the house in order before the hot weather arrives. Optimism seems to be in the air, without the usual amount of lethargy after Christmas when people have to return to work, some with very little money and long weeks ahead through the cold, wet, sometimes miserable conditions. Families tend to be thrown together whether they want it or not, situations occur and the effects can last for weeks until suddenly, as if a cloud is lifted, everyone starts to feel better. Perhaps there is some relief that passing into the New Millennium was less awesome than anticipated.

Life goes on, Marie, and I have a true horror story which you may find hard to believe.

With winter illness in focus and the health service under pressure, a practising family doctor has been found guilty of murdering patients by injecting them with diamorphine when they believed they were having blood tests. The doctor lived as a respectable husband with a family of four, attending school parents' evenings and scout meetings, so the evil core of this man was undetected for years. He injected the lethal dose, somehow covered up the sudden death and encouraged the relatives to arrange cremations. He may be responsible for the deaths of over a hundred people dating back to 1985, but the number of victims may be many more.

This man was allowed to continue for so long because patients and relatives have trust in a doctor in practice. The clean, bright surgery which many people visited created an atmosphere of sanctuary, where health problems could be discussed and, hopefully, cured. Patients gave themselves up, in faith, because we have all been conditioned from childhood to trust our doctor . . .

The evil was uncovered when the daughter of one of his patients found that he had forged her mother's will and the truth began to dawn. The doctor was partly self-destructing as his forgeries were bound to be discovered. He had had an obsession with drugs as a young man, injecting himself, we are told, until his veins collapsed, but still he continued with his family, and his wife is committed to standing by him . . . This monster, shrouded in respectability, took years to uncover.

This case has brought about changes in the medical profession. The General Medical Council here now have to inform all health trusts of a GP's criminal and disciplinary past, and it will be more difficult in the future for doctors to hoard drugs, and more counter-signatures will be required for cremation forms. Some good will come from this tragedy, but this is one of the facets of life that brings such sadness. I hope that I shall soon be able to write to you with happier news.

In mid-January I feel the 'cloud' has not yet lifted and the surrounding atmosphere feels as if recovery from the changeover to the New Millennium is not yet complete. The winter surroundings with bare trees, white-grey sky, which has stayed the same for two weeks, and the raw, cold air has not helped the flu sufferers. There has been a flu epidemic and the hospitals are stretched to the limit; operations have had to be postponed to deal with emergencies.

We, as a family, have survived this phase with colds but, for the first time in years, we seem to have developed some immunity to the flu viruses this year.

Until I write again,

Yours,

Jayne

18th January 2000

Dear Marie,

There is a subdued quietness in the air, winter lethargy now and general disbelief that many predictions for the New Year, did not happen. I can monitor the work pattern by the amount of traffic. A steady flow of cars begins about 6.30 a.m. until 10 a.m.; it is then peaceful again until, like clockwork, at 4.30 p.m. it all starts to flow 50 metres from our house beyond the hedge. I can almost tell the time of day and whether it is a weekend by the traffic. I feel part of a community and being a fair distance from the house – the road is little more than a lane – there are no noticeable fumes from the vehicles to spoil the pleasant reminder that we are a small village.

The days are now a little longer, by ten minutes per week, and there will be a lunar eclipse on 20th January at 3 a.m. I shall not be watching as a cloudy night has been predicted and the moon will appear orange, if it can be seen.

In spite of thinking I should now turn to a liquid diet to reduce some of the weight gain at Christmas, I, like most people, feel a little drained of energy, probably through lack of sun. Generally speaking, good food and a little chocolate after dinner, more comfort and even more enjoyment than usual, seem to be important to compensate for the rigours of the winter. These natural remedies to health and happiness seem to be the best, providing one is sensible.

Kate and I are now focusing on the Lawn Tennis Championships at Wimbledon in the summer and we filled in the necessary forms to request tickets for the Centre Court. I must confess I was not certain whether I wanted to travel there in the midsummer heat, when the television coverage is so good. However, we were lucky to be allocated very expensive tickets which are not transferable. We shall go in spite of the heat because we enjoy Wimbledon fortnight and we would be reminded of our lost opportunity whenever we heard the power of the aces against the racquets.

A week later . . .

The winter lethargy is now turning to calm diligence. The days are cold and bright with more sun than we have seen for many years. We have more daylight and the crocus bulbs are coming through, showing that the depth of winter has left and the new season is beginning.

The United Kingdom is 200 years old this year but no-one wants to celebrate; we are still reeling from the Millennium.

Kate is planning a tour of Italy to include Pompeii, the Pope's summer residence, Amalfi on the coast, Napoli and Capri, and the boys are working on their careers with the same degree of focus which seems to prevail everywhere at the present time.

I am pleased to say the London Eye is now turning and taking passengers, who can view most London landmarks, but there has been another huge setback in the Irish situation. After hours, weeks, months of talking, the newly formed power-sharing Government has been suspended because the IRA will not surrender their weapons. This is very sad for the Irish people, who believed that after years of bombing and murder, they had reached a stage where peace in Ireland was a little closer for them. The subject of surrendering the weapons is so important to the deal that they believe, quite rightly, that no business is better than bad business.

The struggle of human conflict in Ireland is still no further forward and yet technology is advancing at an alarming pace. I heard this week that it is now possible to order goods from a shop in Paris on the Internet. Girls on roller skates collect the orders, which are then dispatched to arrive within a week. The only criticism at the present time is that the Internet picture does not show the texture and quality of the article too clearly; size is also slightly misleading on-line. However, this is certainly the way forward for many people who have neither the time nor inclination to go shopping.

The arrival of computer technology has similarities to the Industrial Revolution of the 1800s but I wonder if our roads and transport system will cope with the acceleration in business.

Yours,

Jayne

30th January 2000

Dear Marie,

Last night, I had the strangest experience I can remember for a very long time but it was pleasant and reassuring.

Michael had a heavy cold, which was one of a series of winter chills which we expect in this environment; in spite of daily fruit and vitamin C, he does not have very much immunity to the viruses and bacteria spread into the air in this closely populated area. The pollution from the motorway three miles away is believed to be contributory to the seasonal 'flu. We do find, however, that if the germs are isolated, the rest of the family have a little more chance of stopping the rampant spread round and round until everyone has forgotten what it is like to feel well.

To this end, I had decided to sleep in the guest room. After a few hours of deep and revitalising sleep, I awoke in the room, which was dark, shadowy and 'different' from what I expected to see at that moment. Spontaneously, due to the size of the room and the position of the bed, I felt as if I had travelled back in time – I was about 14 or 15 (a little older than when we were friends) but the strange, uncanny but delightful feeling was that I actually *felt* like a teenager physically and in good health. I would not have believed it possible through the passage of time to return to that physical state. I really believed that I was in my bedroom in my parents' home; it was small, with a dressing table in the corner, the window overlooked the roof tops and I felt warm, safe, happy and secure. I indulged in the vivid memory of being 15, with wonderful parents and family, happy in my school and music studies, and I could see my mother's face looking in to check that I was all right. It was so moving.

Then I started to think if I had known then, at that age, that my life would develop in the way it has, I would have been thrilled and I doubt that I would have done anything differently.

Everyone's life unfolds in its own way but one thing is for sure and that is that every child deserves a 'good' life and I believe there would be less trouble in the world if we could all trace our lives back to happiness and security in those early formative years.

Yours,

Jayne

3

Memories

Dear Jayne,

I have more time today and it is a real pleasure to read your interesting letters, but then you and Vivienne George always won the needlework cases at the end of term!!!! Seriously, you must be a natural, prolific writer.

Referring to my earlier letter, I cannot tell you how sad I was when I first arrived in Australia. At eight years old, one's cries are listened to and pacified – but adults make the decisions and children fit in. The wrench was unbearable at first; I was physically sick and inwardly sad but I had to think of my father and 'Boss', whose difficulties were worse than mine, making a new life in a developing country.

There were many times that we talked about returning to England, as if comforting ourselves that it could be a possibility but Father felt he had to face the challenge, having taken the family to the other side of the world, rather than face up to failure. So we all became very supportive to each other and made the best of those early years.

After three years, we moved to a larger house in Sydney and I went to the local high school, eventually studying art and design on a full-time basis. It has been a lucrative career and I am 'at home' in Sydney nowadays but I shall never forget England, particularly as my brothers are living in Dorset and Richmond.

Ralph and I were married in 1966. Michaela and Olivia fulfilled our happiness together when they were born in 1972 and 1974. We moved to the large family house in Sydney in 1976, where you located my whereabouts. It is too big for me alone but my memories are in this house and I rely implicitly on Mrs Lawson, my housekeeper. She takes care of cleaning, laundry, shopping and sometimes cooking if I have a dinner party for friends or certain clients. I enjoy cooking but if I work until 6 p.m., Mrs Lawson provides me with a delicious, home-cooked meal.

I am an avid reader of books and newspapers and the local library is my 'second home'. I also teach art at the local High School on two afternoons each week.

Another interest of mine is photography. This began as a tool for my drawing to give proportion, perspective and ideas generally. I sometimes drive into the outback with friends for a weekend, staying in the remote motels, riding and taking photos of anything which interests me.

Apart from this, my daughters visit for birthdays and as the season changes. Michaela has a daughter Rachel who is five years old and Olivia's daughter Bliss is two. They have busy lives and I am committed to my work, which is mainly conducted in my office, two miles away from my home. My little sports car takes me to and from the office.

I cannot tell you, Jayne, how pleased and excited I feel to read your impressions of what is happening in this era and your own family life. I am now looking for your letters *every morning*; they take me back in time to those early years which we spent together, and I can visualise the days at Chetworth School, so many years ago.

Until I hear from you again.

Your dear friend,

Marie

13th February 2000

Dear Marie,

Thank you for your last letter. Like you, I frequently think about Chetworth – perhaps it was because we had our lives ahead of us then or maybe we just remember the very happy times.

I shall never forget your auburn ringlets bouncing over your shoulders and your brilliance at drawing horses. I was so astounded by your talent that, at least once a day, I would ask you to draw a horse; as if longing to draw another, you would pull out your pad and pen and bring one 'to life' with confident, accurate but carefree lines which created an instantly recognisable horse, poised to gallop away, out of sight.

Daily bargaining and swapping of beads and curios at playtime was another passion at Chetworth. Your large stamp collection, however, took up most of our time and I shall never forget the day when you were told you were leaving England. Tearful and confused, you gave me the stamp album for safe-keeping and this was the beginning of my reasonably impressive collection of stamps, which I still have today from working in export for so many years. Mailbags full of letters with stamps from overseas arrived every week and I frequently reminded myself of the way we handled our stamps with tweezers to avoid marking our latest acquisition. The mint collection, which was unused, was our pride and joy.

The stamps stimulated our interest in the countries overseas, which, I suppose, is quite surprising now, considering we were only eight. I still have concern for the rest of the world, hence my horror over Kosovo.

I also remember that your mother, my mother's cousin, died when your family were all very young and your father married a lady whom you referred to as 'Boss'. I could not

50

understand why you called your mother, as I thought of her at the time, 'Boss', but I can now see that she was, obviously, in charge of you all and it was fun rather than hate.

Today's news, Marie, is that this month has been the sunniest on record and dogs and cats are in the news here. Passports have been issued for dogs and cats but the system will not be fully working until April 2001. Eighteen dogs and one cat have been computer chipped, arriving at Folkestone and launching the passports for pets scheme. The pets, arriving on the Euro-tunnel train from France and the ferry at Dover, would normally go into quarantine for six months. This is wonderful for their owners and the pets. I must say I laughed when I heard that their departure had been delayed by bad behaviour, not by the dogs, but by the photographers trying to be the first with the pictures! With microchips checked and vaccine papers in order, they were allowed to enter the country but vaccinations had to include rabies, parasites and worms; without these, they were barred from travelling. What a good idea!

From dogs and cats to the jungle and the Iwokrama rainforest in Guyana, which our Prince Charles is visiting. We have impressive photos of him in an eagle-feathered headdress, happily at ease in the million-acre protected jungle which has been declared a conservation area since 1996. The Guyanese people try to make a living from the rainforest without destroying it and Prince Charles is encouraging organic farming.

But what about Mozambique? The people are clinging to trees to escape from flooding over the entire country . . . It is ironic that parts of Africa are starving through drought and this area is flooded – an era of extremes. The local people have lost everything and their only chance of survival is to sit in trees, awaiting the arrival of South African helicopters; some families have been stranded for days but, again, our Government will be sending money, helicopters and inflatable boats. American cargo planes are conveying food and clothing and Germany and Portugal have offered money and help from charitable sources.

To highlight one amazing incident – a young African woman who had been sitting in a tree for four days gave birth to a baby. A rescue team lowered an army medical officer into the area who was able to cut the cord, winch the baby into the helicopter and then collect the mother, who was shocked and exhausted. Incredibly, when she reached dry land, she walked away from the aircraft with the baby. About a million people arc homeless and thousands have lost their lives.

I shall have to finish writing here today, Marie.

Jayne

20th February 2000

Dear Marie,

Do you ever think about age? Age, we are led to believe, is an important factor in our lives and a number of our decisions are based upon it but I have doubts that this is the right criterion on which to make a decision.

Having an older sister, for what seemed like forever, I was told I was too young to go wherever the older friends were going, too young to wear make-up, to go to bed late, or call adults by their Christian names, 'but your day will come'. So for many years I felt too young to do anything I would have liked to do. My sister, for whom I have affection, was at a different stage with an age difference of seven years. The gap was huge throughout the early years but this started to level out when we had homes and families of our own.

The early seeds of this sisterly affection were sown when

52

I was about four years old. Aunt Bethany invited Esther and me to stay on a farm belonging to her late husband's family in Suffolk. Aunt Bethany was in her early twenties when her husband died whilst serving in the RAF during the war. My father was away with the RAF, stationed at various bases in the UK, but my parents thought it would be safer for Esther and me to go to Suffolk, away from the towns. Up to this point, we kept busy 'spotting doodlebugs' as they came over the roof-tops. Do you remember those German planes, Marie, which droned overhead, then the engine cut out and we tried to locate the position above in case we were the next to be bombed out? When the skies were quiet again, we would collect up bedding and everything needed for one night to make the routine journey to the Anderson shelter at the bottom of the garden. At twilight, the door of the shelter would be firmly shut and it would not be opened again until dawn, when we were quite prepared to see the house in ruins and pieces of shrapnel in the garden. Did you have an indoor or outdoor shelter? At one point, we were told the authorities were digging out the dead at both ends of our road . . .

So the decision was made to send Esther and me away to Suffolk. We were chauffeured away and did not return for several months. My mother had a friend staying with her and between them they carried on the war effort at home.

I will return to the subject of age, but in the meantime, let's continue with our adventures in Suffolk. It seemed to be an extremely long journey, but we were very young, which may account for our impatience. I realised we were getting close to the farm when we arrived at Ipswich, which in those days was a market town with a unique character and I loved the atmosphere and relaxed demeanour of the local people. We drove on from Ipswich and eventually arrived at a rambling old farmhouse with fields and out-buildings as far as the eye could see. The two elderly owners greeted us, a Mr and Mrs Stanfield, who had two sons, Robert and Philip, the brothers of my aunt's deceased husband.

Then it all began for me, the holiday of a lifetime. Ella and Henry, the grandchildren of the Stanfields, were four and two years of age respectively and from the time we arrived we went everywhere together. Esther was always about and could often be seen looking in our direction to see if everything was all right; but we did have fun . . .

I mentioned in my letter the early seeds of sisterly affection were sown when I was about four years old and I think it was apparent at the time of the following incident that we were devoted sisters. If one of our games had gone sadly wrong, I would not be writing to you today.

Esther, Ella and I had time on our hands one morning and we wandered round to a pond which was green with algae and smelled of stagnation, but we thought it looked pretty and offered the prospects of fun. The pond was more like a lake, in proportion to our size. We strolled round the 'lake' with the whole day ahead of us, and how true is the saying 'The devil makes work for idle hands'. An old, disused rowing boat was moored at the side. Esther said she would give Ella and me a ride. We didn't stop to think and climbed in. Esther pushed us out and through a slight movement in the water, although it was mainly still and quiet through lack of current, we eventually reached the middle. At that point, the boat was at the end of its serviceable life through an undetected hole in the side and Ella and I were sinking. Neither of us could swim but we did shout. Esther saw what was happening in the distance and called out words of comfort. She ran round the edge of the lake and I can imagine the sudden panic she felt, but I was surprisingly unconcerned, with an infinite faith that everything would be all right; perhaps I was also aware that any slight movement through panic would be the end of

54

both of us. This was my first experience of the presence of God, and possibly minutes from drowning, an unusual aura of kindness and calm surrounded me which made feel safe and reassured in my desperation.

Within a minute or two, Esther found a frayed rope which was conveniently long enough to make a rescue attempt. She tried several times to reach us with the rope and to this day I can see her mustering every conceivable idea to deal with the crisis. The water was too deep to wade out and the boat was sinking fast but Ella and I were still calm with a belief that we would be saved although we could do nothing about it.

The exertion of trying to catch the rope rocked the boat and made matters worse; what was left of the old vessel was wobbling with every movement and desperation led to desperate measures; Esther threw the rope with such a force, as if given the strength of Samson, that Ella managed to catch it and my sister pulled her in. I was left alone but with the positive thought that I was next.

I was standing on what seemed like planks of wood, sinking to above waist level when, with a great thrust, the rope arrived and I caught it. I was weak with fear at this point that the next stage would fail, but I managed to hold on and Esther pulled me in.

Ella and I, shivering with cold and fright and covered in green slime, appeared in the kitchen of the farmhouse; the family were shocked and we were led away for a good wash down and a hot bath.

Esther, trying to create some fun, actually put our lives in danger but also saved us, and the vision of her pulling me to safety at that formative stage cemented our relationship for years to come; I wanted to go everywhere with her, be with her and live her life at that time.

In the following weeks we rode Wild West rodeo style on some wonderfully healthy pigs. Two dear horses called

Promise and Beauty gave rides for the little ones up and down the country lanes surrounding the farm. Esther swam with the ducks in a not-too-clean duck pond but I vividly remember her falling from top to bottom of some very basic granary steps, from which she felt the bruising for years. The granary was full of chaff to the level of the door at the top of the steps; this made an irresistible romping ground for us three little ones. For some reason, we didn't sink to the bottom but that was something we didn't think about in our excitement.

Other vivid memories were running barefoot across the large, frosty floor of the dairy where butter and cheese were produced. Home-made madeira cake and drinks were offered for 'elevenses' although meal times were very difficult for me; there were only certain foods that I enjoyed – everything else led to a daily confrontation with these kind people. While I was trying to explain my lack of appetite, they were trying equally hard to feed me as a child should be fed.

This gave me a good insight into how to treat my own children many years later. After the first week, an unpleasant medicine was spooned into me on a daily basis which I was told was for acidity – I did ask to see the bottle, which had a familiar name, but the subject of food remained my only problem with these kind, dear people.

A pale blue, square and very thick diary was sent to me by my mother and her friend and somehow holding this diary gave me the reassurance I needed that I was right to speak out about food which I could not tolerate, so far away from home. I loved the pale blue, leathery feel of the present, the gilt edging and the interesting printing inside the book which taught me, with some help from my aunt, the days of the week, months of the year and numerals. Above all, I loved the diary because it was a present from my mother and her friend. I did not realise the significance of the gift until years later, and even now I turn to my current diary all the time.

Another lasting memory was being shown into a small, dark study lined with bookshelves, to speak on the telephone. I loved that room – it was so full of interest. I will never forget the telephone, having to hold the main stem in my left hand and balance something like a tube with a flared end to my ear.

At night we climbed rickety stairs to the maid's quarters, where beds with starched sheets were made up for Ella, Henry and me. Aunt Bethany used to check that we were all asleep about 8.30 p.m. but baby Henry would never go to sleep and it was the same every night, until he eventually gave in; we all awoke at dawn with the sun usually streaming through the tiny windows.

Sorry, Marie – I was talking about 'age', which has a bearing on our lives from childhood. From time to time, our age comes into focus and it seems that many people become programmed in their minds into thinking they cannot do what they would like to do because of their age. With the exception of prejudice in the work place, surely the most important factor is how we feel and how much we can cope with. Any age can have a new beginning. Any age can be beautiful or handsome – it comes from within.

Coincidentally, the London Marathon has just taken place here, which illustrates that too much importance should not be placed on age. The oldest runner this year was Abraham Weintraub, an American who is 90 years of age, and he completed the 26-mile course. That is truly amazing. Roger Black, a silver medalist in the 1996 Olympics, was overtaken by a 65-year-old woman. Millions of pounds are raised for different causes and every year it becomes more entertaining with clowns and runners in fancy dress; an eight-man team portraying a London bus completed the course this year.

Computering, gentle aerobics, dancing and visits to the theatre etc. are all available for the noticeably 'younger' residents of nursing homes nowadays. Less smoking, some healthier foods, medication and social services are probably contributory to this new lease of life.

Marie, what do you think of cloning? I believe cloning cells has been researched to treat diseases in elderly people such as Parkinson's disease, Alzheimer's and diabetes, and seems to have endless possibilities relating to the ageing process. My personal feeling is that no-one should stand in the way of progress, providing that progress does not distort mankind. We are told that man was given free will and there will always be striving to learn and develop beyond our present state. Let's hope it is beneficial in the outcome.

Until I write again,

Jayne

26th March 2000

Dear Marie,

I hope you are well and enjoying my news and views. I said to Michael, 'When I write to Marie, it is like going into the inner sanctum of life and time', while he is lost in his world of business.

Today's news is that Kate has now returned, safe and sound, from her tour of Italy. The Vatican in Rome has such atmosphere, as we could see on her video; the height, the marble and the craftsmanship of centuries ago are far removed from the modern era. The buildings in Pompeii tell a story of their own – the tourists in the video are rooted to the ground, peering at the ancient ruins, perhaps wondering how these people worked without modern tools and equipment – yet the craftsmanship and skill were evident, and we can still witness the ideas and approach to building at that time. The most significant feature seems to be the lack of accurate measurement, compensated by the strength of the structures which have survived through hundreds of years. The buildings, although crumbling through the passage of time, are being preserved for the interest of visitors and the Italian people of today.

Kate returned home refreshed from her holiday and she is now planning to do more touring. Jules and Peter have aspirations about holidays in America. Largely due to the American films, like most young people here they think of America as the most advanced country in the world, but we try to give them a balanced view. One reads about a six-year-old girl who was shot and killed by a seven-year-old boy because they had an argument the day before. The boy found the gun lying on a bed at home and it seems his father and grandfather are already in prison on gun charges. The boy is too young to be punished but the owner of the gun will be charged with manslaughter.

Life in America is a different culture and young people need briefing on the crime and violence through the availability of guns. Racial problems are a huge issue, with the American police being criticised for their handling of situations, yet the Internet gives instructions for making bombs, so it is doubtful that guns will be taken in, for the fear one may be replaced with the other. Schoolchildren have been particularly at risk in recent weeks but, thankfully, television coverage, videos and the media help the young ones like Jules and Peter to make educated decisions on what to expect.

It is a glorious, sunny day with some blue sky, cloud and cool temperatures, which is inspiring for the early month of March, and today I have been thinking in depth about people rushing here, rushing there, with such purpose and incentive and I wonder, when I see them bustling in all directions, what it is that is giving them the will to drive them on.

My own personal 'get up and go' factor is and always has been 'achievement'. Getting the family mobile in the morning with tea and breakfast and ensuring a happy family is ready for work; completing a list of jobs for the smooth running of the family home are, in a sense, an achievement. In a personal sense, most of my interests emanate from school life; the subjects I have an opportunity to study and the ones in which I am interested have come to the surface and, from that foundation, there is always a subject to pursue for further achievement.

Children get up and go to school for interest; young adults go to work for interest and financial gain. Older adults create homes and families, but when families have grown up, there is a new phase of life, simultaneous with retirement, when it seems important to be resourceful and strive for achievement using past learning, talents and experience.

To illustrate my point, Kate, Jules and Peter are now adults and apart from running the home, which has become easier with time, I am now 'picking up the threads' of my education by giving more time to playing some of my favourite music on the organ and redesigning the decor, quite apart from having more time for motor-cruising on the south coast. Achievement with the sweet smell of success has to be one of the greatest incentives to the human race.

Whilst thinking about achievement, we see four people on television every day, at the moment, who are the candidates for the Mayor of London. They are all achievers with a motivation which can bring success and a purpose in life. The Mayor of London will be elected in May, whilst at the same time, the elections are under way to vote for a new American President. Following the primaries, as I'm sure you know, the race to be President will begin shortly between George Bush, Republican, and Al Gore for the

60

Democrats, to replace President Bill Clinton towards the end of the year. This is a level of achievement which stands alone; these people offer themselves to lead their countries and that takes a certain confidence. Can you imagine, Marie, waking up one day and realising you are the Prime Minister – conviction must be the strongest motivation.

I have not achieved my goals, in the last week in March, as anticipated in the winter and this makes me feel there is too much work and pressure all the way round. I feel overpowered at the moment, and in times like this, there is only one way to resolve it; I turn to pen and paper and make plans for a better system and probably more help. Sometimes, just to go out of the house for a few hours makes a vast difference to a seemingly impossible situation. My problems are relatively minor but somehow they can still be overpowering.

My sympathy is with 25,000 people employed in the car industry in Oxfordshire and the West Midlands who are facing redundancy. The BMW company is selling off Rover and unless a venture capitalist can save the company by producing a new mini car, these people will be unable to find work in the area. This will lead to social problems on a huge scale.

We are told that the hi-tech billionaires are going to change the world but people are resilient to changes and I think the fundamental issues of human existence with the family unit will always triumph. Let me know what you think about hi-tech Marie.

With the news that billions of pounds are being provided for our National Health Service and education, income tax is to be increased and the stamp duty when buying a house will be more expensive, the supporters of the Labour Party will not be disappointed. It is encouraging that inflation is low at 2.5 per cent; a good life is achievable in this country, providing people work hard.

Thinking about the family unit – today is Mother's Day. I am not too sure what will happen as last year the young ones slept through it. Jules was staying at Kate's flat, following a very late night in her area; Kate was tired and neither of them responded to my lively suggestion about having lunch together. Peter did not know it was Mother's Day but Michael and I were happy to celebrate the occasion. Every suggestion I made was turned down for one reason or another and general apathy finally overruled the early enthusiasm. Somehow Mother's Day, I feel, should include the children, so as they could muster only insufficient interest, we called it off and they happily went back to sleep.

The day progressed to evening. Kate brought in a lovely yellow chrysanthemum in a wicker basket and a beautifully worded card and message. Peter had also organised a card and chocolates, which made me feel very spoilt because he had thought about it himself and put them on the table in front of me, rather than losing the idea and apologising.

Michael and I agreed to go to Jules's club where, with a plethora of electronic equipment and a microphone, he entertains up to a thousand people at weekends. Suddenly, and totally unexpectedly, Jules dedicated a beautifully worded message over the microphone to his own very dear mother.

Whilst the family circle is important and I felt very spoilt, we also encourage our young ones to have an outgoing interest in people and the world in general to keep a balanced outlook.

Jayne

Dear Jayne,

Your letters remind me of those wonderful times when we were discovering life and what it was all about – memories which had to be put to the back of my mind, which I am now enjoying again. I learned to forget through necessity but I can cope with them now because I am free to do something about them.

I must confess I did cling on to my school satchel when we left England, which included a jigsaw, some books and my pencil case; I have kept the jigsaw and books, perhaps subconsciously hoping that that phase had not gone forever.

I enjoyed hearing about Mother's Day. I had a phone call from my girls and their little ones. As I have had to live a professional life for 20 years, most of our anniversaries are celebrated by a phone call, which is all right. Now to answer your questions about how I would feel if I awoke one morning to find I had to run the country as Prime Minister. Well, Jayne, that would be all right but the only aspect I would resent would be my loss of freedom. That is very important to me and I would feel 'caged' if I were unable to go from A to B without the company of a bodyguard or photographers.

You asked me what I thought about the hi-tech world. Being an artist, I do not have a natural aptitude for computers but I have a fully fitted office in Sydney with the most up-to-date computers. Two girls run the office; my home, which is two miles away, is also somewhat hi-tech. I have found it essential to move with the times and to a large extent it is progress, certainly from the times when you and I played with an old manual typewriter. But the next generation, who will be 'weaned' on computers, will be the converted.

Keep writing, Jayne.

Your friend Marie

Dear Marie,

So, here is today's news.

Snow, sleet and flooding all over the country are causing concern in April, our springtime. The weather patterns are extraordinary, but my sympathy is for the African people at the present time. Parts of Africa have not seen rain for four years and we are told 16,000,000 people are starving through drought. This has been happening for years and large areas of Africa will surely become barren waste land, whilst Mozambique is flooded. Another tragedy is disease, with Aids spreading through the continent as if out of control.

Black Africans are now rioting, overrunning and slaughtering the white farmers in Zimbabwe, which became independent 20 years ago (we remember it as Rhodesia). President Mugabe is claiming that the white farmers are trying to reverse black independence and he wants land reforms to eradicate the white 'master'.

We all have a place in this world, and with respect, all people and races could live harmoniously to make the world a better place, but fighting causes more anger; discussion and compromise is a better way forward.

Speaking of harmony and co-existence, here is an example of what we do for love . . .

Peter has taken a job working for a four-star hotel. We are very pleased that, whilst hoping to secure a job in the airline industry, he has now taken up some full-time employment. He says he has 'goals' to fulfil and I admire his determination to succeeed. There is only one downside at the moment and that is that Michael and I are involved, as we are both called upon to drive Peter to and from the hotel; not that we mind helping the young ones, but we really do not have the time to give, with our own work.

Peter has a scooter and he is willing to take it to work but we are uneasy about the distance involved – seven miles – in the fast traffic. Having grappled with the dilemma, I have decided to drive him to work at dawn.

The mornings are lovely for this short season. The daylight breaks through and the energy of the birds feeding gives me the feeling that this is the time we should all be beginning the day. However – having completed the early morning routine and taken Peter to work – tiredness starts to kick in and it does seem to be a very long morning to me; my mind does not work the same and my physical output is simply non-existent so, in fact, it is virtually non-productive. This state has been slightly improved by having a long lunch break, nevertheless, repeating the exercise at 4 p.m. seems to break into the whole day. We are doing this to give as much support to Peter as possible to begin a career, whilst waiting for a position in the airlines. As parents, we give our help to the young one who needs it most at the time.

The options are to be chauffeurs or encourage Peter to take driving lessons.

When I feel low with tiredness, it has passed through my mind that parents have donated kidneys for their families, so who am I to complain and how sacrificial is the power of love.

The flooding is now subsiding and I have just noticed that walking on a fine day in April before 10 o'clock is so refreshing and invigorating. I should have known this, but one sometimes overlooks these very wholesome pleasures. The winter is retreating and the air has a unique freshness after months of keeping warm indoors. I find it clears the thoughts and emotions whilst energising the limbs for the day ahead. The air has a purity, pollution allowing, which is cool and uplifting but it can be short-lived with showers, which are, of course, a feature of this month here.

Following on from my appreciation of the spring, one is also aware of horses being exercised and this reminds me of your artistic brilliance, which I felt at the time was similar to that of the great artists. Imagining wild horses running, galloping, thundering into the distance, for the sheer joy of releasing pent-up energy together, with the same physical needs, heralds the beginning of this exciting season, for me.

Many people obviously feel the same way when this joy is experienced by thousands, if not millions of people, through television coverage of the Grand National race at Aintree. The superb Papillon was the outright champion this year, owned by Ted Walsh and ridden by his 20-year-old son Ruby. I am sending some dramatic pictures of the event to you.

The excitement of the last furlong of the race, with horses and riders striving for competitive satisfaction and enjoyment and then receiving their pats and sugar lumps from excited owners, has to be seen to be fully appreciated. What a pity we cannot go together, Marie.

Another thrill this week has been the royal photo-shoots at Klosters, giving us much appreciated graphic updates of the young princes William and Harry.

Outdoor activities now take us into the heat of summer when, for most people, the daily routine has to change. How did you and your family adjust to the high temperatures in Australia; I have been told they reach 109 degrees F? Cold showers, swimming pools, electric fans, sensible nutrition, cotton clothing and working at certain times of the day must help.

It is Easter here now and, apart from the religious aspect, which we give thought to each day, it is a holiday which puts an end to the winter for me.

This year was all that it should be; we packed for an overnight stay at Chichester, which we think of as our second home. Many years ago we found a country route which was quiet at holiday times, through interesting rural villages and farmland.

We drove for just over an hour to our yachting club, where we were greeted with the usual chorus of seagulls gliding and hovering overhead. Lunch was ready to be served, by the sea, in a setting on a par with a stately home. Although a little early in the season, the weather was warm and sunny and the weekend was a tonic for Michael and me.

We returned home by the same route and we both felt ready and happy to face up to the problems we left behind. Back to nature, an inexpensive weekend and holiday breaks are such a good idea. How do you relax, Marie?

Until I write again,

Jayne

17th April 2000

Dear Marie,

I have had an embarrassing experience but I think I handled it correctly.

Our local sports club was holding a summer ball, which was widely advertised in the village. Michael, Kate and Jules were optimistic that it would be an interesting and, hopefully, enjoyable evening, but Peter had other plans. We bought four rather pricey tickets for Kate, Jules and ourselves and the men checked out their dinner jackets.

On the evening of the ball, we took photographs in the garden and then made our way to the club. We actually arrived an hour before the dinner, which I think, on reflection, was too soon as there were groups of people gathered around whom I felt would rather not be disturbed as they seemed happy with their own 'clique'. However, to my relief, there were some people I knew from the 1970 era (I think I mentioned that we had recently moved house, returning to this area which we left in 1982). All was well until we checked the table plan and made our way across the floor to be seated. Immaculate pink cloths adorned the tables and sparkling glasses, shiny cutlery and flowers completed the setting, but my feeling was that it was all terribly formal.

Introductions were made and I felt pleased that Michael was on my left side and Jules was on my right side, with Kate on the other side of Jules. At least we had one another to talk to.

On Michael's left side was a highly made-up party animal called Cynthia. It is often said that it takes two to tango but this was an exhibition unsurpassed in my experience. Cynthia briefly acknowledged me as Michael's wife and then went to lengths to explain that the man she was with was a friend of 30 years – there was nothing between them and she was a divorcee. Throughout the entire dinner, Cynthia, who I could not help but notice had very angular features exaggerated by harsh make-up, demanded Michael's attention. Being a gentleman and a good talker, he went along with it and may have felt just a tiny bit flattered by the attention. I chatted to Jules, then Jules changed places with me and I chatted to Kate. The man on Kate's other side said nothing, except, 'Why did Jules change places with me?' as if to imply that Jules preferred the company of Michael, which was not a very good start to the evening. The other guests sat staring into space looking uncomfortable as if they were wishing the whole situation was a bad dream. This went on for an hour throughout the three-course meal.

After the meal, Kate and I went to the ladies' room. When we returned, Michael and Cynthia were still deep in conversation so we sat for a little longer and then I said to Michael, 'Kate and I are going to get some air,' which he acknowledged. We went to the balustrade and I said to Kate, 'We do not worry about this sort of behaviour when we have been happily together for 30 years, as a relationship becomes stronger and these hiccups are usually short-lived.' A younger person of Kate's age may see it as the start of a breakdown in a relationship which may lead to anger or tears.

After our little tête-à-tête, we returned to the hall and by this time the music had started. I must confess, I was tempted to go straight into the dancing but, somehow the 30 years we have spent together made me think twice and I decided to walk across the floor to tell Michael first. I received a lovely smile from Cynthia's companion and Michael jumped up as if in sheer relief to get away. We went into the dancing and watched a display of limbo and Cynthia was never seen again. I cannot help thinking what a foolish person she was – her companion had been totally neglected and would probably not accompany her again and Michael never gave her a second thought. However, it could have caused an argument between Michael and me.

My belief is that one should try to talk to people on both sides as much as possible but it is astonishing that this sort of behaviour is not uncommon.

Well, my dear, time has caught up with me, so until I write again.

Jayne

4

A Dream or Reality

Dear Marie,

We are now awaking at dawn with the birds. The mornings are bright; the trees are bursting into colour and the blossom is fading with a scattering of pink and white across the lawn. Rennick, our elderly gardener, complained that it was making him more work, but he will be retiring next month, so I shall forgive him. The temperatures are now soaring to 70–80 degrees F, and to sit in the sun for ten minutes only at the beginning of the season is pure luxury. It is cool in the morning and cool again at about 7 or 8 p.m.; we are feeling the heat; it is not unbearable but the work plan has to change. Coffee and tea breaks in the garden help to build a suntan, which we still find fashionable here nowadays.

We have all had an incredibly busy month. Jules entertained a hundred people at a wedding near the coast as the party co-ordinator. This work relieves the bride's family of the responsibility of ensuring the guests enjoy the evening, while at the same time providing a musical background. Michael helped him and they found themselves wading through mud across a field in the early hours of the morning – luckily they have a sense of humour and laughed their way through it. Peter is still working at an hotel until

70

his chosen career becomes airborne, and Kate is on holiday. To add something to the present build-up of tension, a bottle of pina colada burst its cork and sprayed all four corners of the kitchen, covering the walls, floor and computers with a fine, sticky film which will take hours to remove. I was the culprit in removing the wire cage from the top and then being unable to remove the cork. The pressure built up and lifted the bottle from the worktop. It flew through the air until it landed on the floor behind the fridge, from where we were able to trace the events of the previous evening. Unfortunately, Inca, our adorable cat, was unable to tell us exactly what happened but she did get a soaking in the process.

Inca is an angelic, intelligent black and white cat. She was born into this loving family of humans and kittens in Kate's underwear drawer. Her mother, Mimi, kept her carefully guarded secret for weeks, although we did wonder why she kept looking round the back of Kate's cupboard, where there was a secret opening to an ideal bed of soft satin and lace. Eventually it became clear why she was so intensely interested in the drawer when three tiny kittens were found; so Inca was born into luxury and she does have a sweet nature.

Inca's mother subsequently produced another four kittens within weeks, before we could have her neutered, due to the lactation cycle, but then there was an unexplained mystery. Mimi went out one Sunday morning when we could hear clay pigeon shooting in progress and she was never seen again. We searched the grounds for days and pinned posters to trees; in fact we never stopped looking for Mimi, so Inca, who is identical to Mimi and the last remaining cat of two litters, has become very precious to us all.

Before the cats arrived, we kept a guard dog called Chieftain for nine years. Mainly due to lack of training in his early years, before our time, he felt unable to allow anyone into the house and felt equally unable to let the family out! To say the least, it was a neurotic time for us all, but in other ways he was almost human and, being part Labrador, the caring nature of the breed shone through.

At medicine time for the children, he would chase them and round them up if they ran away. He could see for himself the difficulties we were having and joined in the team. Chieftain was often found with Peter in the pantry, helping Peter, who had a small appetite, to dispose of food he could not swallow. At other times, particularly at week-ends, he guarded Michael's newspapers with a heavy paw as if they were pure gold and only Michael was allowed to touch. He very quickly learned the difference between parents and children, so we let him take charge of us all.

Other news is that we have a London Mayor. Ken Living-stone won the support of the majority and our capital will now have the special attention of the London Assembly. This is such a good idea to create coordination and I hope London becomes an even better place as a result of this decision.

A new baby boy called Leo has been born this month to Cherie and Tony Blair, our Prime Minister. The baby is the first to be born whilst his parents occupy 10 Downing Street, London, the official residence of the Prime Minister.

The motorcar and airline industries here are having serious problems. Rover cars have been saved from closure by BMW. British Airways have suffered losses of £200 million through competition and increased running costs.

David Coulthard, the Formula 1 driver, crashed in a light aircraft, but he was able to walk away from it, and the champion jockey Frankie Dettori also crashed when his plane plummeted to the ground. They both survived, so miracles do happen.

The long summer days are now helping to make life

easier; as it says in the song: 'Summertime – and the living is easy'.

Kate and I have decided to drive to the beautiful park and school which I moved to after you left for Australia. The setting was chosen by Henry VIII to build a palace for Anne Boleyn, which you probably know was 450 years ago. A mansion now stands in the park, with a stone from the old palace built into the wall at the north entrance. We decided to visit the mansion again as my niece Jenny is getting married there in the autumn.

Our journey was quite straightforward, only 20 minutes from home and better signposted than the old days when I cycled into school, and yet, Marie, believe me, when I arrived at the entrance to the park, it seemed just like yesterday that the young girls in their blue and white striped dresses, navy blue hats and blazers, mostly with new bicycles awarded for successful entry into the school and satchels or cases brimming over with books and pencil cases, were filing into the school for the 8.45 a.m. start. They, probably, all have grown-up families of their own now and I wonder if they made the best of that first-class education.

Kate and I parked the car and walked into the mansion, where tea and home-made cakes were on sale. The atmosphere is still medieval and I think Kate enjoyed the afternoon sun and the change from her office. We ventured into the mansion, where the rooms for functions have been sympathetically restored in regal colours with highly polished wood. Kate waited by the door as she was concerned that it would slam behind us in the wind and we might be locked in over-night. We were very impressed with the venue for Jenny's ceremony and reception and at least we can drive in all our finery to the wedding on the day, without delay . . .

Today's news is that Jules is learning car mechanics through experience – his starter motor engages seven times out of ten, but when it stops, it seems to be in the thick of the rush hour or late at night. Michael comes to the rescue with his 'jump' leads and Jules has been very helpful in calling a taxi at night.

We have open house at the moment, with builders coming and going to provide the extra bedroom storage which I had so much fun designing to suit our special needs. One tends to forget that there is much preparation for these wonderful schemes. Having cleared the room and hovered on call whilst work was in progress, clothes, shoes, bags and dozens of forgotten items had to be checked, dusted and put back, which took some time and energy.

Rennick retired in midsummer, so the necessary interviews, selection of a new gardener and the presentation of an encyclopedia of plants and flowers took place. Thinking about what has been happening in our quiet moments feels more like a dream when everything has crowded in from all sides and suddenly you wake up in relief.

The most difficult day was last week, when I tried to start the Jaguar and it seemed completely dead. Michael replaced the battery and it seemed fine, until I reached the local traffic lights, taking Peter to work; the car shuddered and started knocking. Peter said, 'I hope it does not break down' – we had six miles to travel. On balance, I thought it would be all right, so we continued with the journey. The worrying part was at every traffic light and when slowing down that it might break down. However, it did keep going. Peter arrived on time, which was one less worry, so while the car was going, I had to do my best to get it home. We have had trouble-free motoring for years with Jaguar and BMW cars and this was a rare incident.

With the heat of the day, the condition of the car deteriorated and I began to feel that it would not reach home. The worst happened when I had cars and lorries behind me, in front of me and at the side, and the engine stalled. I had a rush of thoughts such as 'This is new, you haven't had a situation like this to deal with, Jayne,' and 'Am I in a friendly environment – how much chaos is this going to cause with a huge car in the middle of traffic? I will now have to phone Michael and bring him away from his work – do these people round me really worry if they are late for their appointments?' Then again, I also felt that there might be a chance, even now.

A spontaneous instinct came into play and I threw the gear into 'park', turned on the ignition and thank God it started. A quick rev of the engine and I kept going until the next set of traffic lights. By this time, I felt like a zombie, which by definition is 'a corpse said to be revived by witchcraft', with pale, stony, wet face in the heat. The final and worst part was circling a large roundabout close to home, really praying until I reached the other side. I have heard it said that God holds you in the palm of his hand, and my prayers were answered for I managed to reach the drive of the house before the engine faded away.

I said to Michael, 'I cannot take that car out again.' The problems were caused by the oil filter, which has now been repaired. All in a day's work.

I have now recovered from my ordeal and I have some midsummer news for you, Marie. The temperatures have been the hottest on record here although it has not been unbearable. We are dabbling around in cold water most of the time with all doors and windows open. Kate sunbathed for an hour with her high-factor cream. I warned her of burning after half an hour and it reminded me of the seventies, when the children had to be checked in their prams. By 9 p.m., with the heat of the day and the fresh air, to be honest, I could not work or sit down, so I retired to bed and it seemed to be daylight until midnight.

It is beyond my understanding how 58 Chinese illegal immigrants suffered, trapped in an airtight lorry from the

Continent to Dover. The air-vent was closed for the voyage and the young hopefuls literally breathed carbon dioxide in hot, cramped conditions, banging on the walls of the lorry with their shoes for dear life. No-one heard them and their bodies, apart from two survivors, were found by the customs officials amongst boxes of tomatoes.

Backpackers in your country must have felt similar despair when the hostel in Queensland was burnt to the ground at night when they were unable to escape. We are getting news that they were sleeping on the top floor of the building which was engulfed with fire, without fire alarms.

I must finish here today. Until I write again,

Jayne

3rd July 2000

Dear Marie,

I have not been able to write throughout most of June; events have nearly overtaken me and my days have not been the same without the early morning exchange of correspondence.

However, some normality has returned this morning and I have so much to write, I am not sure where to begin.

Kate's 29th birthday was last Friday, which she celebrated with friends in the New Forest. Tessa and Will organised tickets for an open-air classical concert, firework display and a birthday cake to be presented during the evening. Kate said it was very emotional when the entire audience sang 'Happy Birthday' to Kate and one other person. She returned at lunchtime on Saturday and we booked a table for five at a local Italian restaurant. As soon as we walk in the door at this particular restaurant, we feel as though we

76

have taken a plane to the Adriatic coast, for example; the food is so authentic. Kate said it reminded her of her happy times in Italy. Everyone wants to spoil Kate – she is so hard-working and self-disciplined and has an appealing countenance.

My journey to buy Kate's presents could have been my last, again centred around my car. My brakes failed on a fast dual-carriageway but Peter and I managed to bring the car to a halt, made some arrangements to get home and came to the conclusion that it was a death trap.

As a result, organisation and method came into play and I have now changed to home deliveries of shopping. A huge order was delivered to the kitchen, which saved so much time. Of course, many people here are already doing this on the Internet, as I expect they are in Australia. Shopping will be more pleasure and less stress from now on.

This morning we have awoken to flooding. I thought we would find a moat round the house following the severe weather and rainfall right through the night, remembering that this is our summer and the weather patterns are always changing. Our nearest neighbour told us on the first day we moved in that he had seen our house, which is below road level, surrounded by water, like a house on an island, and I wondered if this was happening again. I have never forgotten his words but equally I have never seen anything approaching that situation, so I will put it down to comments which people make . . .

Three days later – The rain has subsided and Kate and I have been to the Wimbledon Lawn Tennis Championships. We drove to Motspur Park, parked in a designated area and were taken by coach into the grounds of the tennis club. Groups of ladies were chatting and drinking Pimm's; there were surprisingly very few men about at this stage. Stewards were officiating; coffee was flowing, strawberries and cream were in evidence and a band was playing, giving the whole area an atmosphere of good organisation and high standards.

Kate was happy to look around while I phoned Michael and then, with a feeling of privilege, I made my way to row L, under cover. As I took my seat, it was as if I had been reading a book and the famous characters in the pictures had come to life, talking to one another, hitting the tennis balls with probably the most expensive equipment in the world, and the colours were vivid. It was amazing to be sitting there, so close to the brilliant sporting famous whom we had only seen on TV.

A gruelling five-set match followed, with Andre Agassi from Las Vegas and your Pat Rafter from Australia. Pat Rafter won the match and this was followed within 15 minutes by Pete Sampras and Vladimir Voltchkov, who lost in straight sets. I cannot remember sitting totally lost in play for five and a half hours, as we were at Wimbledon. Kate and I arrived home two happy people after a very enjoyable day.

Visiting veterans and champions of the seventies and eighties are here this year to celebrate the Millennium.

Your Mark Philippoussis, known as the 'Scud' for his powerful service, has beaten our Tim Henman, and Martina Hingis, who was expected to win this year, has been beaten by Venus Williams from California. Venus and her sister Serena seem to be strong, aggressive, awesome, dedicated and full of youthful stamina.

Just in case you haven't seen the final results; Venus Williams was ladies champion, winning her match with Lindsay Davenport, and Pete Sampras won his match over Pat Rafter. Pete Sampras has now won the Wimbledon championship seven times and created a new record with his thirteenth Grand Slam title; he achieved this record with tendonitis and pain from a back injury, for which I have subsequently heard he has received acupunture treatment. He seems to excel through his power, stamina and accuracy in placing the ball in the court. It is not surprising that with this being a record-breaking year, with his parents and fiancé present and his tough match against the brilliant Pat Rafter, that we saw the emotional side of the champion, when he dropped to his knees at the end, fighting back the tears.

The plans for a roof over the Centre Court will help the continuity of the matches but, as yet, rain still stops play. We were still too young at Chetworth to know whether either of us had any sporting talent but I think my particular problem was lack of agility. Netball, hockey and ice-skating were more rewarding.

We had our first experience of sleepwalking two nights ago with Peter. Michael and I went out to dinner and Peter ordered a cheese pizza at home. It came from a different restaurant from usual, with generous amounts of cheese, herbs and spices. Since Peter has become an adult, he has a strong stomach for rich Indian and oriental food. However, during the night, Peter rose up from his bed, left his bedroom, walked along the corridor to Michael, who told him to go back to his bedroom. He obeyed and settled back into his sleep. My theory is that because I had been out all day with Kate, in his subconscious mind he was checking that Michael was there and he was not alone in the house, as Jules works very late. Perhaps the cheese inhibited deep, normal sleep but my main concern was the stairwell at night which, fortunately, he subconsciously avoided.

A week has elapsed and we haven't experienced any more walking about at night, but the nights are very short and the weather pattern has changed again from almost premature autumn to midsummer conditions.

There is a sense of excitement, incredulity and happiness uplifting the country as we begin the celebrations for the Queen Mother's 100th birthday on 4th August. I am beginning to feel the strength and positive outlook coming from this wonderful lady as she prepares for every official occasion until her birthday in just over two weeks' time. She has always emerged as an example of courage, having a sense of duty which is such a fine example. The younger royals have had difficulties; their different characters and situations have not always contributed to making the right decisions.

How lucky we are to have this fashionable lady in our midst to lead us with all her qualities as she did in our childhood, Marie. She was always there, the mother figure, seemingly indestructible. To see her re-emerging is so encouraging to us all and, hopefully, it will do wonders for the Monarchy.

Our Prince William is 18 this month. I feel so thrilled that we have a handsome, clever and very charming young prince to continue the work of the royal family.

The beauty, colour and excitement of Royal Ascot has been brought to us through the excellent TV coverage of these events. I am sorry that blue jeans and casual wear bordering on scruffy have become the norm over the last few decades, but Royal Ascot just takes us back a little to the days when men and women dressed elegantly; men were more protective and the ladies a little more subservient. Women needed, in many ways, to have a better life, be more educated and independent but with this emancipaton, there have been worrying results; whether they are contributary or otherwise, the institution of marriage has been threatened, there have been more savage attacks on women and the moral behaviour of society has lowered its standards. However, I am indulging this week in visiting this spectacular racing event, although this year it has been extremely windy and cool, making it less pleasant than usual.

Leaving behind all the worries of past and present generations, we have heard that a 44-year-old Wiltshire businessman called David Hempleman-Adams is the first person to fly solo in a balloon over the Arctic Ocean to the North Pole, and he also made the journey in record time. With his radio communications failing with the team on the ground and the autopilot not working, it was necessary for him to stay awake. Apparently, he very nearly aborted the flight, fearing that he would disappear or perish as the early pioneer Salomon Andrée met his fate in 1897. In this Millennium year, we have the advanced technology but the vital element which no-one can control is the weather, so it appears, balloons, ships and even planes are still at risk, particularly with human error and mechanical failure.

The Little Ships have been crossing to Dunkirk harbour to commemorate the evacuation of hundreds of thousands of soldiers from the beaches of France and Belgium during the Second World War. Fifty-eight of the original ships crossed from Dover and it took eight hours to reach France, where they met an appreciative but noisy reception. I sometimes wonder how our parents' generation lived through those years – there was very little counselling for stress but they did smoke cigarettes, pipes and cigars, which has proved to be a killer in itself.

While we are revelling in the summer events, it makes me aware of the racial fighting in Zimbabwe, which I mentioned in my earlier letter. President Mugabe is inciting black people to kill the white farmers and drive them out of their homes to gain complete independence for the country. I am not sure that this supports the peaceful co-existence which is expected by all nationalities in this country.

I shall have to finish this letter very soon, but there is just one other bit of news which is unusual and the cause of some hilarity amongst everyone involved. A new bridge has been built to span the river Thames, which represents a blade of steel in the new Millennium. However, when it was eventually finished, after its opening, hundreds of people lost their balance and felt dizzy and nauseous whilst crossing from one side to the other, as the bridge was visibly wobbling. The designers and engineers have been called in to correct the wobbling walk-way and it will, therefore, be closed for a few weeks.

Well, Marie, this is all I have time for. Jules is on holiday for two weeks and Peter is at home due to a clash of personalities with the hotel manager, so until I write again,

Yours,

Jayne

15th July 2000

Dear Marie,

Some schools and colleges have broken up and I vividly remember the days of July when Kate, Jules and Peter were children. There was always a huge effort made for the end of term sports days, fetes and prize givings, knowing that a long holiday would follow. All sporting equipment had to be freshly laundered, if not replaced and new items such as running shoes acquired; parental support was needed for the school fetes in providing items to sell which were invariably home-made, as well as a personal appearance on the day at difficult times. The prize-givings were not always a joyous occasion but I, naturally, wanted to be present for the children. On the last day, the same precise time-keeping had to be observed and I was never quite sure if the young Peter would go to school being a child who resented discipline. Having surmounted that hurdle, they were collected again at 12 noon. It is little wonder that mothers with children have very little time for anything beyond the care of the family; but parents are given this enormous inner strength to deal with almost all eventualities relating to their children, providing they are safe, well and flourishing.

We would all arrive home at lunch time and the end-of-term reports were produced. Our teachers were masters of the art of understatement and one felt work must be done in the holidays, but the atmosphere was lost and by the end of July, school work was put aside and we took up our own methods of education, with shopping trips to conquer the concept of money, newspapers laid strategically about the house to encourage reading, talking in figures as much as possible and particularly involving the children in the art of conversation.

The pressures of school timing were relieved but holidays away from home had to be arranged for us all to feel better for the break. I thoroughly enjoyed those years, in spite of the tireless effort, aggravation and some worry which is usual with growing families. Perhaps you have a tale to tell when your girls were growing up?

Marie, this was very rare when you and I were children but child abduction is increasing in this country. An eight-year-old child disappeared whilst playing with her sister and two brothers. They were playing around the trees in a field, as every young child should be free to do without danger.

She was never seen alive again and two weeks later her naked body was found ten miles away. How can the parents, numbed and distraught with the truth, tell their other children without leaving them psychologically affected in their formative years? I believe that it cannot be adequately explained and, therefore, the killer has damaged the lives of the whole family and the relatives. How vulnerable we are, but one must stay positive.

Discussions are taking place here on whether child sex offenders' names should be published in newspapers. If this were to happen, inevitably mistakes would be made and some innocent people would be hounded by the public for varying reasons such as mistaken identity and location. Secondly, it is believed the publication of offenders' names would send them 'underground', putting children in greater dangers.

Children and many other people are at risk in the community whether offenders' names are published or not, and it appears that every area has offenders, so I believe the problem has to be tackled in a different way. Policing and social services cannot adequately keep track of known criminals, who have to be allowed back into society when they have served time. Perhaps there should be categories, ranging from one-time offenders to maladjusted and hardened criminals. This is where, I believe, the probation and counselling services should be developed and strengthened to categorise the offenders and regular contact should be maintained, based on a medical report. Whatever system is employed, I believe children and their families should be protected, not the criminal.

A small team of retired people and parents with mobile phones, drawn from local residents and working to a rota, could fill an important role in this respect. The scheme would have to be well co-ordinated but I think it could be the solution to child safety during the school holidays. It would also encourage children away from the TV and computers, which are safe alternatives to playing outside, but which have inevitably led to obesity amongst the young.

Maybe walks in the woods, parks and along the rivers and towpaths should be made by families and friends in groups until the world becomes a better place.

Your friend

Jayne

4th August 2000 – the 100th birthday of the Queen Mother. How wonderful that this glamorous lady is like a very much loved mother to the whole nation.

Everything stopped for two hours. The Queen Mother appeared with Prince Charles, who has escorted her throughout her birthday celebrations, at the gates of Clarence House, her home in London. She enjoyed a march past by the King's Troop Royal Horse Artillery, the band of the Irish Guards and the Queen's Guard. She then received a laser printed card, which has replaced the centenary telegram from the Queen. This was delivered in a Royal Mail van by her personal postman. A chair was brought out for her but she stood throughout the march past in high-heeled shoes, on sticks, following her fairly recent double hip operation.

The gates of Clarence House were closed behind her and we then saw her with Prince Charles in the open carriage decorated in mauve and yellow, which are her horse racing colours, leaving Clarence House to travel very slowly to Buckingham Palace for lunch. The sun shone knowingly and the crowds were ecstatic. Many people were interviewed who had come from America and Germany; some visit this country every year for her birthday and all declare their undying love for this lady.

At 12.30, she moved onto the balcony at Buckingham Palace with the Queen and Princess Margaret to the sound of music below and it was, to quote the words of a commentator for BBC television, 'a tearful occasion'. Slowly, the balcony filled with members of the royal family and I really felt at that point how important they are to this country. There will always be differences in people but the main core of the family are good for us.

In well-judged timing the Royals left the balcony and we

understand the celebrations continued throughout the day and evening.

The day was an inspiration to ageing people – God bless her.

15th August 2000

Dear Marie,

We are now in the midst of the quiet, lazy, humid days of August. The lanes have become bridleways again, children's voices can be heard all through the day, shouting and crying when tiredness takes over. Mothers are making their way to parks and picnic areas and the humidity is like a force of gravity pulling against you if you dare to work. The heat makes every effort harder until, by the peak of the afternoon, one just irritably gives up. This is happening every day at the moment and I can see why a large percentage of people do not work at all during this month. Of course, you will be fully adjusted to these temperatures now, Marie, and perhaps the heat in Australia is different.

I also have a habit of soaking up people's problems like blotting paper. This is all right providing one does not finish up blotting paper with all the effervescence of one's personality flattened by concern. Whilst trying to recover my positive state from listening to problems, which is my own fault because I like to know what is happening and whether I can help to overcome difficulties in the lives of the children, I find myself analysing their make-up and the right way forward.

Kate is capable and independent. I can only hope that her future will be secure.

Jules is a son to be proud of and I hope he finds the niche he is looking for in music and business.

Peter is popular, particularly amongst the academics, outgoing in personality and, again, when he finds his way in business, there will be no turning back.

I must finish this letter now. Although it is a little cooler today, the heat will build up again in an hour or two so I will now have to deal with some of the essentials in the running of the home.

Yours,

Jayne

17th August 2000

Dear Jayne,

Like you, I am weary of work, meeting clients and sorting out problems, so I am taking a very short break on the coast for a few days. There is much to explore here and one tends to see so little in the towns. I really 'wish you were here' but that would be too much to expect. Perhaps one day it might be possible.

With love,

Marie

19th August 2000

Dear Marie,

Thank you for your hurried letter from the coast. Do you take many short breaks or do you prefer to get away from it all for two or three weeks? We prefer the former as the 'recovery' time is quicker. That is probably a strange remark but I believe one can reach a point of relaxation where it seems almost impossible to work again straight away. We also tend to stay in this country – we haven't flown since Kate was born ... which brings me to the tragedy of Concorde.

For me, Concorde was beyond the realms of human error. It was an aeroplane which, with a seemingly untarnished record, would fly forever. I feel sadness and disbelief that my trust has been taken away in that beautiful, marvellous model of human engineering.

Have you heard that an Air France Concorde crashed to the ground and burst into flames just outside Charles de Gaulle airport in France? We are told that the pilot had requested maintenance to be carried out on one engine before take-off. As the plane left the ground, the control tower saw flames coming from the port side but the pilot was unable to reverse take-off. Although it will take months for a full report to be made, there were a series of catastrophes resulting from the fire and Concorde crashed, killing everyone on board and several people on the ground.

This particular incident is a setback to people with a fear of flying, but let's face it, participation in flying and boating will always be an act of faith. My own first flight was in a DC6 troop plane chartered to fly over the mountainous region of France to Spain, arriving at Perpignan. Most of the flight was subjected to turbulence, lightning and thunder, with cabin signals flashing orders and general chaos till our feet touched the ground, but some of my work colleagues said, 'Yes, we sleep through that sort of weather.'

On the ground, Peter and Kate recently visited the Farnborough Air Show in Hampshire. This sort of display of aviation expertise including stunt aircraft twisting and turning in the sky, the sheer power and deafening noise of the aircraft engines and the precision of the Red Arrow aerobatic team, amongst others, can only leave one gasping in incredulity; thus restoring one's faith in what can be achieved in reaching for the sky. As one inhales the fuel amongst a sea of video cameras, it is clear to see that every second counts and it is almost too much to comprehend the brilliance and courage of the pilots performing in this way. It serves to commemorate this time in history, in parallel to the medical and scientific advancement.

One can reach for the sky, as we did for the Millennium, but sometimes we fall short of our dreams. I am referring to our Millennium Dome, at Greenwich. It cost this country over £700 million and it has been sold this week for £105 million, to a company who will convert it to an amusement park but, in the meantime, the proceeds of the sale have to be used to keep it open until the end of the year. One immediately thinks of the impoverished inner cities and other environmental needs which still exist. It is, of course, easy to be wise after the event; there was a volcanic build-up of emotion in this country prior to Y2K for a splendid monument to be created, to our cost.

We are not alone in our problems. Fires are raging through the west of America, moving from state to state. One million acres of trees have turned to white ash due to the parched summer and lightning strikes. Firefighters and planes overhead treating the inferno have been unable to contain the fires, which, it is believed, will be burning until the snow arrives in October.

The balance of nature on our planet is always there if you look hard enough. It was only recently reported that deadly mosquitoes have been found in America. Could it be possible that the fires will exterminate them?

A week later – Humidity is still bearing down, but there have been showers to cool the atmosphere. We have Jenny's wedding at the end of the month, for which a few shopping trips will have to be made. Have I mentioned that Jenny is Esther's daughter? Her wedding is on my mind a lot of the time, and my feelings of excitement have motivated me to get on with everything, even more than usual, and there is also a certain fear that all may not go as well as expected on the day; I will live with this in the weeks to follow. Esther and I have a sisterly bond which I suppose is important to me to keep intact and, therefore, I hope that some silly incident does not cause bad feeling. The geographical distance between us allows for certain respect to be maintained and yet when I see her, I sometimes think the years of separation have been a waste of a good relationship.

With my Aunt Bethany, the distance is even greater. I am always hopeful that everyone will get on well together and be happy but, sadly – perhaps I am partly to blame (but unintentionally) – it is not always so easy to achieve. For my part, my open mind becomes disillusioned with the actions and remarks of others, but nowadays I do not retaliate. Years ago, Esther and I argued over our beliefs, feeling in some way pleased that we actually had a point of view on which to argue. Mother used to look from one to the other, nodding in approval that we could debate a subject with conviction. Although our meetings are now infrequent, I would tend to think very hard before I speak, certainly not argue. In this way, we shall stay friends as well as relations.

There are five days now until Jenny's wedding and I still have the strangest confusion of feelings about it from which there will be no freedom until afterwards.

I feel enormous pleasure at the thought of seeing my god-daughter, Esther and Rupert and not too worried that anything will go wrong that cannot be laughed about but, I suppose, I am worried about the emotional effects throughout the celebrations from 2 p.m. to midnight. Whilst I am concerned about this, I should be thinking about the other guests and, in fact, Jenny, who may be coping with worse problems. These occasions can be an ordeal as well as joyful and one has to prepare for it in this way. Here, my thoughts return to the royal family, who are managing these situations, probably on a weekly and daily basis. How we turn to them for guidance and an example.

The strain and knotted emotions make me wonder whether formality will give way to informality as time goes by. There are already signs of this happening in the City, where the immaculate City gent in bowler hat and pin-stripe suit is rapidly disappearing from the offices and more casual wear is acceptable. In fact, as far as I am aware, one only sees the bowler hat worn nowadays by the order of the Orangemen marching in Northern Ireland. If people feel better and work better, it seems logical to make the change.

The air has cooled slightly – a freshness we had almost forgotten was possible. This has happened simultaneously with heavy carpets of hailstones falling in Yorkshire and a freak tornado this week in the North of England – we are in August and no-one here can remember this before.

There is also a mood of helplessness everywhere over a Russian submarine called the *Kursk*, which was involved in a freak accident in Murmansk. It is believed that an explosion ripped through the craft and more than a hundred submariners were drowned as the flood water filled the vessel. Are you getting news of this!

This particular accident has touched a nerve for me. As I believe I have already mentioned, Kate took part in underwater diving. Her training made me aware that there are more risks involved than one would realise. Most of the crew of the *Kursk* were young men in their twenties with their lives ahead of them and the scenes below sea level must have shown panic, drama, fighting, resignation to the inevitable and eventually quietness on the sea bed;

then the horror felt by their families through an accident which was probably never believed to be possible. I have to say to myself that the media inform us of most of the news and, therefore, we have to take it all and, hopefully, learn from it.

The makers of Concorde have learned from the recent disaster; all Concorde aircraft are now grounded, having lost their licence of airworthiness; that is so sad.

Marie, I do have some fun news for you today which has caused some hilarity here. Wild bears in America are making their way into the towns and taking food from whatever source they can find, as it is easier for them to do this than to hunt in the wilds. They are intelligent and have seen that man has an easier life than their own. I have heard that the dingos in your country survive in a similar way but have been known to kill babies and children. I must confess I am concerned about Inca when the foxes are hunting here. This brings me, again, to fox-hunting, which is another subject for much thought.

I shall have to finish this letter now, Marie, but I will write again in a few days.

Yours,

Jayne

Tasmania 12th August 2000
(received 26th August)

Dear Jayne,

I am writing to you from Tasmania. I made a sudden decision to leave the office girls in charge and take a much needed rest. I have made several trips to the island over the years. I may have mentioned it before but photography is one of my main interests nowadays. It is a great tool for my art-work and I am planning to go to the lakes and rivers of Tasmania on this trip.

I shall be there for three weeks but I will be looking forward to reading your letters on my return.

With love,

Marie

3rd September 2000

Dear Marie,

I hope you are in good health following your trip to Tasmania; that was obviously longer than a short break and many thanks for the outstanding photos of the island.

It is now three days since Jenny's wedding. Two days of numbness, emotional levitation and inevitable strain have meant that full work output has been put on hold, but today I feel fully charged, in fact, a little overcharged, and this has given me a deeper insight into stress. Radiant health can make one a little too zealous – oh dear.

Michael, Kate, Jules and Peter were exemplary in their timing for the wedding arrangements and supportive in every way. I feel so proud of them when they sense the importance of a situation and react quietly and efficiently. Jules had three engagements on the same day, one before and one after the wedding, but he made it to all three without complaint or query.

Michael, Kate, Peter and I arrived at the beautiful park and grounds dating back to medieval times, which I believe I have already mentioned was the setting for my chosen school, after you left England. A trio played classical music until Jenny's arrival. She looked stunningly beautiful in white with a tiara resting in an abundance of tight curls. The bridegroom, Edward, also handsomely attired in morning suit and gold waistcoat, wiped away a tear as Jenny stood beside him. I felt the love between Jenny and Edward and it seemed as if everyone else in those surroundings was there just to complete the occasion for these so obviously happy people.

There are so often differences between families which cause seemingly insurmoutable problems but if there is a strong love, it is of no consequence, is it?

The wedding ceremony went well, the speeches were explicit and humorous. Cameras were clicking for over an hour and much filming of the day took place. This was followed by a feast along banqueting lines; then some exercise was taken in the beautiful walks surrounding the mansion. As evening fell, fresh food was brought in and music for dancing filled the mansion.

About ten o'clock, having signed a book of good wishes, we felt it was time to depart. Following eight weeks of build-up to such an occasion, one cannot return to normality over-night . . .

The gradual unravelling of ourselves from Jenny's wedding, which is now a week ago, has left me with a need to break free and explore the coastal areas. I have already mentioned our 'second' home at Chichester. With limited time, we can reach the marina in just over an hour, with a traffic-free route through the country; there are seventeen miles of inlets to explore, with slipways for boats to enter the water and quaint little cottages painted in pastel shades. The local inns, chandlers' and shops cater for the tourists and there is an abundance of flowers in baskets, good food and drink.

As soon as we arrive at our yachting club, cheery smiles greet us and there is an atmosphere of healthy well-being. Suntanned athleticism abounds and there are pockets of people in every direction getting on with their particular task, whether it is preparing to release a boat into the slipway, mooring up to come in, cleaning down, winterising their boats before the season changes or purely having fun.

There is such a spirit of good friendship, in the main, give or take one or two exceptions. People are generally happy and this encourages comradeship. Complete strangers are like lifelong friends when manoeuvring their craft. At the end of the day when the boats have been moored, there is much technical explanation of boat handling and navigation. Laughter is generated from funny incidents and daily encounters and all this takes place at the clubhouse, over a drink, in an atmosphere of great excitement and even expectation of what will be happening tomorrow.

We have been members for 13 years. We have the academics and professional people wanting to get away from it all, and there are always, of course, the seafaring mariners who know their boats, the tides and the treachery of the water; it has been said to us more than once, 'Master the sea, or it will master you.' In and around the harbour, providing you keep to the correct side of the buoys, follow the charts and tides and know your boat, it is incredibly exciting.

It all began in 1987 when we were on holiday with the children, looking out of the hotel window, whilst having dinner, at the idyllic scene below. Sailing boats and small craft were gliding proudly through the waters. It looked interesting and tranquil. Business was booming and we were unanimous, as a family, that Michael should buy a motor boat – the time seemed right. He had said on many occasions he would like a power boat; we had photographs of him manoeuvring a small craft when he was 16.

The following day we drove to Poole and selected a power boat. Michael handled the business; we climbed into the boat and were shown how to switch on the engine. The salesman vaguely waved in the direction of Poole harbour, which is the largest natural harbour in the world, and at a speed of 5 knots, we steered out to sea.

On reflection, our naivety could have led us to tragic circumstances, but many, many first-time buyers of boats are put in the same position. Kate, Jules and Peter were 16, 13 and ten at the time and still needed adult supervision. Gradually we realised what we had taken on. The winds, tides and currents have the most control on a boat and the power of the engine has to be used with and against the elements. However many expensive boats there are to the portside, starboard side and ahead of you, you cannot just 'stop'. This is an obvious remark but it is not something one thinks about until you find yourself 'on the water without a brake'. The locks are some of the most difficult situations to negotiate due to the proximity of the vessels and some skill is needed to come through without incident.

Returning to the day in Poole, we were in the middle of the harbour without life jackets, a boat-hook or a fender (a large hard cushion designed to protect the side of boats). In a way, ignorance was bliss; we had no idea of what may have happened. Michael kept cool and in control. On entering the marina, the wash took the boat towards the wall and Kate, with her youthful strength, leaned on the wall with her arms to keep us clear, whilst the boys and I guarded the bows, stern and portside.

The final test of skill and endurance came when mooring within inches of other motor yachts. We were luckier than we deserved and no harm came to us or the boat, but that was a day we shall never forget when thinking of what might have happened. On returning from holiday, we stopped at the Chichester marina, joined the yacht club, and a couple of friendly members helped us to bring the boat round the coast. We were moored on the north bank for several years whilst taking various courses on boat handling and navigation and gaining the radio-telephone operator's licence.

We laugh at it now and even experienced yachtsmen arrive at the club with stories of gruesome encounters and adventure at sea . . .

For some of us, there is an addiction to the sea, sunshine and coastal areas but this year, our long-awaited plans for the summer break have to be put back. From time to time, we book into an hotel to have a rest. However, support for racing at Goodwood has resulted in all hotels within 20 miles of the area being fully booked. Michael may also have to be hospitalised within the next month and the weekly tests beforehand prohibit making too many plans. However, all is not lost, as we can visit our club at any time. Providing the winds are not more than a force 3, all types of weather can be fun.

The autumn school term has now begun and it is bad news for the parents as our roads here have very nearly come to a standstill through protests against the price of petrol and diesel. Tanker drivers have formed a blockade against fuel leaving the refineries, claiming that the tax on petrol is too high. It has been put up consistently in previous budgets. Petrol stations are not receiving their normal deliveries and panic buying has led to the pumps running dry. It has taken less than a week to disrupt the nation's work and food supplies, but the essential services have been able to continue, albeit to a lesser extent than usual.

Urgent talks have been held with the people in power at the refineries but the Government has made it clear that they will not change their policy on the price of petrol as laid down in the budget because of protests and blockades – that is not the way to govern a country – but they have reassured the nation that deliveries of fuel will be made within hours. The Government has sixty days to appease the lorry drivers and farmers.

London's new Mayor, Ken Livingstone is supporting the Government and urging people to use bicycles and walk as the weather is good. The price of fuel, road congestion and air pollution is a serious issue here. It will be interesting to see how it is resolved in the next few years.

Discussions at dinner parties, certainly in the local pub and occasionally in TV documentaries suggest that man will take to the air in the pursuit of speed. There would be huge potential in your country, Marie, but, with the overpopulation here, there would be new dramas of flying over towns and villages and the organisation would have to be impeccable.

Heavy rainfall, flooding, thunder and lightning have driven sleepy wasps and battalions of Daddy-long-legs indoors. Perhaps you do not remember the crane flies which invade us here in September. The garden shrubs look richly green but the lawns have a covering of autumn leaves. Darkness is falling at 8 p.m. and there is some talk about Christmas creeping into family conversation.

Two days have passed and there are more problems at the Millennium Dome. Apparently fraud has been discovered and I cannot help feeling some annoyance and disbelief at the newspapers this morning which photographed a long queue for petrol following a radio DJ's innocent remark about a possible impending blockade of the refineries.

Disruption on the roads, at the petrol stations and in the shops last week has been followed by a localised power cut today which lasted six hours. We were warned that essential work had to be carried out but, nevertheless, there seems to be one aggravation after another. Candles, a portable radio and gas have saved the day and, admittedly, it is better to be without electricity now in the autumn than in midwinter. Perhaps we all have it too good nowadays and I really should not complain.

On the positive side, an irritating wasp sting has now improved, passing through the painful sting, like an injection, which lasted for two days, to the intensely itching stage, which also lasted for two days. It happened late at night so I spent a semi-wakeful night wondering whether there would be an allergic reaction, particularly as it is 20 years since the last one. However, all is well, but they are little demons and I cannot imagine, and try not to think about, how the Africans cope with the mosquitoes which inject malaria. They are large and deadly and I have heard this week that much of Africa is falling victim to the disease.

I am writing to you by candlelight during a power cut and I feel a little like Jane Austen or Charlotte Brontë may have felt at that time. Over the years we have moved on from candlelight; it has that innate fascination for us all and sooner or later we are drawn, possibly through primitive pleasure, to bring it back into our circle.

Kate is busily following the current trend for candle therapy. There are candles for every mood and design, and a display brings her friends together to look, analyse and pursue the ultmate decor for their homes, with the nights closing in. The calming and energising aromas are very effective and the perfumes are pleasing.

Years ago we were also mesmerised by coal and log fires, seeing images, feeling inspirational, romantic and even judging the frosty conditions outside. Fire inspired musicians as in de Falla's very descriptive Ritual Fire Dance. Primitive man was able to build fires, gaze into them, keep warm and dance round them. Then changed to the use of electricity and central heating for cleaner air and conditions, but sooner or later the primitive pleasures return in one form or another.

Jules has told us that he would like his own home, base, 'pad' or whatever – yet again another primitive instinct on reaching maturity. This is the goal he is trying to achieve in happily working all hours. We talk over dinner, otherwise there is a cheerful chorus of 'Hello Jules', 'Goodbye Jules' night and morning – such is the pace of life.

Peter's 'primitive' urge is physical fitness and self-defence. He has risen up the ranks according to the colour of his belt in karate, tai kwondo and tang soo do. I watch with motherly pride as he does his displays, with aggression, across the kitchen floor and commend him on preserving and improving upon his youthful fitness.

So we all have our primitive instincts, Marie. From primeval existence to modern medicine – Michael and I have an unspoken understanding between us that everything is 'on hold' for a while until he has had a rectal operation, which is due to take place within a few weeks, following painful and embarrassing bleeding. Waiting for this is creating a gentle calm in the home, while we speak reassurances to each other that it will be good to get it cured and begin the recovery period back to full health. It is an unpleasant episode in our lives, but we have to go through it.

Reluctantly, I shall have to finish this letter here.

Yours,

Jayne

7th September 2000

Dear Jayne,

I am now back in Sydney and I have never seen so much activity and organisation taking place since I arrived in Australia. The town is overflowing with tourists, to such an extent that droves of residents are leaving the area in fear that the railways and airports will come to a standstill during the Olympic Games, which have not been held here since 1956. The organisation has virtually taken over and disrupted the city, but it was thrilling when the Olympic flame arrived.

Of course, the young ones will benefit from the Aquatic Centre, the new attractions on Bondi Beach and the Olympic Park. We shall just have to adjust for a few weeks until the city returns to normality.

Good wishes to you all.

With love,

Marie

10th September 2000

Dear Marie,

I felt the excitement and growing euphoria about the Olympic Games which are starting in Sydney in a few days' time, as described in your letter which arrived yesterday.

You have obviously settled in well with the Australian temperament, which I see as generally calm, easy-going and friendly. With the choice of Sydney for the Olympics, the dynamic Aussie, it seems, has taken over to make this the biggest party ever known.

The build-up seems very similar to what we were experiencing last year before the Millennium. Sadly, our Dome project has gone badly wrong and by the time it closes at the end of this year, it is expected to have cost £700 million. It has been said that the public have not supported it well enough, but the amounts are huge, Marie. Some vital factor was obviously missing in the project and it appears to require specialist research into what will make people travel, view and be present at such a venue that cannot be missed or ignored. The contents of the Dome, it appears, did not have the winning formula . . .

Ten days later – In late September, we are enjoying sunshine and rain intermittently; the weather patterns are so well balanced at present that, unusually, the garden hose has not been used at all this season; that indicates that we are getting far more rain than usual.

I have been following events at the Games and I have the greatest respect for the magnificent show you have staged for these Olympics. We are pleased with the British effort – I think we are, at present, up to ten medals, but it is, indeed, sad that drugs have again marred the games. I believe one brilliant athlete was suspended after taking a cold remedy. This is an aspect of sport which, in my opinion, needs to be controlled more efficiently for the sake of everyone . . .

I have now heard that our British team returned to England with 28 medals – 11 gold, 10 silver and 7 bronze – which was, apparently, the best effort since 1920 when it was held in Antwerp, Belgium. I can imagine the excitement in Sydney now with residents returning – some getting down to work and others having a holiday to recover.

Since I last wrote to you, there has been an improvement all the way round here; petrol is available and the traffic is moving again. This dispute has coincided within a few days with the Prime Minister giving his speech at the Brighton Conference to placate the party and the general public. He said the Government had realised, with hindsight, that they should not try to run tourist attractions; pensions will be increased and there will be continuing investment in the health service, schools and public services, but it will prob-ably take ten years to make the improvements required here. There seems to be a general mood of acceptance at present.

There is also much success and good news. I am thrilled

and feel a sense of relief over the revolution in Yugoslavia and admire the ordinary people for fighting to restore the country to its former glory. Deposing the leaders and calling for democracy will result in the lifting of sanctions imposed against them after the recent wars in the Balkans – they should now begin to recover from their ghastly ordeal.

The time is drawing near for Michael's operation on 12th October. We are both going through varying feelings of nervous anticipation, but the rectal haemorrhoid has led to so much discomfort for him over the years that it cannot come soon enough, whatever we think or feel. At intervals throughout the day, his hospitalisation comes into my thoughts and I have to say to myself that he will be in good hands – this helps considerably – and, it should be better for him for the rest of his life when the healing stage is complete. These phases in life make one feel there is no time to be complacent or bored; work at what you enjoy and enjoy your life . . .

12th October 2000

I am writing today, Marie, because it is today that Michael will have his colonoscopy and operation. I am feeling strangely calm, almost as if I have to accept what comes next without question. His bag is packed and he is taking purgatives and clear fluids. I am just keeping busy without any normal planning of the day as I have to take him to hospital at 3.30 this afternoon.

Kate visited last evening for dinner and whilst Kate and I were quietly nervous and tense, the boys and Michael found the whole business of colons a huge joke. Jules, Peter and Michael spent most of the evening laughing about the subject, which had a very good effect on Kate and me. I remarked to Kate that I have learned more about the male gender since the boys grew up than I had ever known before.

Jules left for an audition, Kate went back to her flat and we all felt better for having spent the evening together . . .

19th October 2000

It is now nine days since Michael's operation and I feel as if I have been out in a boat on a choppy sea – happy but inwardly churned up. I am happy because Michael's operation was successful and he came home six days later but, inevitably, the days, although planned, have been different – a little as if I am not sure what to expect next; there is more to be taken care of but I have achieved less than usual.

We have all suffered the pain with him; he does seem to have a low pain threshold, but we have confidence in the doctors and nurses, and with modern painkillers, the suffering is probably bad but bearable. Patience throughout his convalescence is now needed, with an optimistic attitude.

I have decided to keep the news of his cousin Sacha from him, which we were told about when phoning her concerning his operation. She has just completed five months of cancer treatment. I thought the timing was bad and she has finished her treatment (it was caught through a routine check before there were symptoms). As soon as he is well enough to take it on board, in a few days' time, I shall let Kate tell him in my presence.

I am snowed under with pressing work, Marie, so I will try to write again soon.

Yours,

Jayne

14th October 2000
(received 21st October)

My dear Jayne,

I hope this will be good news for you. Your letters have had such a profound effect on me that I just feel I must book a flight to England and re-trace those early years. I shall stay in London where I can promote business but I will, of course, visit you when it is convenient and hopefully see Roderick, Malcolm and their families. Perhaps we could even go back to Chetworth and our old family homes. I am enclosing some recent photos.

My plan is to come for the whole of December and perhaps a week in January.

Let me know what you think about this.

Marie

23rd October 2000

From Jayne's diary

There is one week to Halloween and I have the strangest mixture of emotions I have *ever* experienced – excitement, fear, anticipation, doubt and, at the same time, just sheer joy and rapture.

I have received a letter from Marie and she would like to come to England in December and see us.

She has enclosed photographs and I must say she is exactly as I knew her all those years ago. Her slim build hasn't changed at all. She grew to about 5′ 6″, and her oval, smiling face, which was always alight with fun and enthusiasm for the day ahead, is exactly the same but showing the character lines of maturity. I shall always remember her skipping and running, never walking, and, above all, she stood out in a crowd with her auburn ringlets, curled with ribbons.

105

My fear, anticipation and doubts are based on whether this will spoil a memory which has always been with me throughout the years. It has been almost fantasy in the way it has been based on all the positive emotions I remember – so many years ago – and the fantasy has grown in my desire for all people to be good to one another – but childhood is one state of mind and adult life is another.

Will we recapture the innocent delight of eight-year-old girls – their joy of being alive, meeting other children and share our love of life again? We both have the experience of a lifetime, which may have changed us. If we have changed, the dream will have gone forever – that is my worst fear.

5

The Meaning of Happiness

Dear Marie,

I have read your letter several times to be sure that I have not just awoken from a dream; I am still not quite certain that it is reality. I am thrilled that you have decided to come to England and retrace our lives together so many years ago. Michael, Kate, Jules and Peter are happy for us and they hope you will stay with us whenever possible.

Events have overtaken me recently, but everything is now under control. Michael was convalescing at home, just a few days after his operation and still feeling very weak, when a friend in the area came to the door and said she had been diagnosed with cancer. Her treatment has been arranged for next week, and she asked Michael if he had been given his test results. Following the news of his cousin Sacha's cancer a week ago, it calls for positive thinking to go into mega-drive on how to support and reassure a patient when all this is happening around them.

Two nights ago, there was a tornado on the south coast at Selsey, which tore across southern England, pulling down trees and causing widespread flooding. It wasn't quite as powerful as the hurricane of 1987 but all night I kept waking and sleeping whilst the winds whipped across Surrey, Sussex and Kent. Each time, I wondered what was to follow

107

– would it be worse, would the trees stand up to the strength of the gales and, in fact, would we survive if one came through the roof? We are sheltered to a certain extent as the house is situated lower than the ground level, with hills all around which act as a windbreak.

Kate was caught up in the flooding when travelling to her work. Traffic was at a standstill, whilst there were small bottlenecks of motorists trying to drive through water. We spoke to her on her mobile phone and at one point she thought she might have to lock up her car and make her way to Gatwick Airport until the chaos cleared; she eventually arrived at work five hours later. Kate came to us for dinner and will attempt the same journey tomorrow. Travelling is difficult at present but, giving due credit to the English, order is quickly restored. Today, the weather is lovely – sunny, bright and dry with blue sky and cirrus clouds, making everything so much more encouraging.

Michael is making good progress now – he is reducing the painkillers each day and routinely consumes fruit. The last two weeks have been distressing; we have made visits and phone calls daily to the hospital and local doctor to adjust the medication and seek reassurance. However, his visit to the GP yesterday confirmed that his tests were satisfactory, and that has given the necessary boost in the road to recovery. I am inwardly weary, which is to be expected, but we now have to keep our homelife ticking over whilst regaining strength all the way round.

Once again, Marie, I am thrilled that you are coming to England in December, and we shall plan a special dinner party for the weekend after you arrive. I shall invite some friends, Andrew and Vanessa and Charles and Ailsa. We see them from time to time and they are good company.

Let me know where you want to stay in London, which will be easier for sightseeing, or locally. We have a train service about ten minutes from here which makes six stops to London Victoria.

The weather is very changeable at the moment and you will probably need clothing for mild and cold weather – coats and rainwear would be useful.

Excitement has turned to planning here, and I am taking on extra staff to cope with the backlog of work created through recent events, before Christmas shopping starts in earnest.

You have probably thought about your itinerary, but a few suggestions could be helpful. London sightseeing, including Knightsbridge and Kensington (Harrods) would be interesting. Obviously, the art galleries, including the Tate Modern, will be important; possibly the Dome and the London Eye, but I have heard this has been affected by the storms. I expect a few days with your brothers will be high on the list and we could possibly return to Chetworth. We would be delighted if you would join us for an old-fashioned traditional Christmas Day and on Boxing Day we have tickets for an ice show to the music of Andrew Lloyd Webber. Can we include you in his extravaganza? It may be a good idea to keep at least a week open for relaxation and overflow of planned events.

Let me know, Marie, what you think about the above suggestions and also whether you would like me to make your hotel booking, with any preference.

Until I hear from you,

Your dear friend,

Jayne

6th November 2000

Dear Jayne,

It seems we are all happy about my impending visit.

I shall stay at the Dorchester Hotel but do not worry about making any reservations; I will organise this from my office here. I like your ideas for the sight-seeing in London and I will be delighted to join you on Christmas Day and Boxing Day. It sounds 'out of this world' and I, like you, can hardly believe this is happening.

Until we meet.

Marie

8th November 2000

Dear Marie,

Many thanks for your letter by express airmail.

I can tell you are thrilled about the trip, which makes me feel that the years that have passed have not changed us; we just have so much more to catch up on. You mention that you would like to go to the theatre once or maybe twice during your trip. Again, I will send to you a list of entertainments and try to secure tickets.

Michael and I will, of course, be thrilled to meet you at Heathrow – perhaps you will let me have your flight number and time of arrival on 1st December.

Although my letters are usually 'a little' longer, today I feel I must get on with plans for your visit, so I will not write another word today and await your news and details.

Yours,

Jayne

From Jayne's diary

I am writing a daily journal until I hear from Marie that her arrangements are in place for her visit on the 1st December.

There is rain, rain and more rain. Parts of Africa would think we are the luckiest people on earth, but the rain and flooding we have had this year is unusual. I fear there will be another winter of anguish for, at present, the average commuter has gridlocked roads, widespread flooding, queuing for petrol due to another threatened blockade by tanker drivers. Insurance premiums will probably be increased due to flood damage and road accidents. Trains are running on cracked tracks up and down the country and a slowdown has been ordered by the Government for safety, which is good.

Yesterday we were flooded up to our porch due to an abnormal rain fall blocking hard-working drains; the falling autumn leaves compounded the problem but Peter cleared the leaves before nightfall.

Travel difficulties were the main issue last week. Michael's car was waterlogged, so Jules and Michael were sharing Jules' Renault. I suggested to Kate that travelling to her office might be easier, once again, from our area; she stayed with us until Monday morning, but returned to her flat on Monday evening. There is no respite from rain at present and there is a constant murmur of motor engines struggling through the 'river' outside the house. We now have waves lapping against the banked verges and the smell of petrol and diesel are filling the air all day.

On the brighter side, we now have a Father Christmas about 18 inches high, swinging his hips to 'Jingle Bell Rock', which I couldn't resist on a shopping trip with Michael and Kate.

We are all very concerned and alarmed for the Queen Mother, who has broken her collarbone; we understand it is very difficult to breathe with such an injury.

General excitement and some chaos is causing a little confusion since we heard about Marie's arrival in a few weeks but I will pull myself together and plan the days ahead to relieve the pressure.

At the eleventh hour on the eleventh day of the eleventh month 2000, the time when we remember families in two world wars, there is a different scene outside. Most of the leaves have fallen, making the garden lighter, and the colour has changed from green and yellow to gold overnight.

I have not heard from Marie as to whether her flights and hotel are now confirmed, so I must confess I feel a little subdued, lacking incentive and slightly numb, but my philosophy is always, in the absence of news, to be positive. I shall continue with my planning and see what happens day by day.

The American Presidential elections are being held, which is focusing our attention here. Voting is taking place for George W. Bush, Republican, or Al Gore, Democrat and Vice President to Bill Clinton, whose term will end in January. George W. Bush is only a few hundred votes ahead at present. However, news is reaching us that voting in the state of Florida has been muddled. American voters have come forward to say that the young as well as the older residents were confused by the ballot papers and, in fact, at the end of the count, unopened ballot boxes were found. They are now awaiting the absentee American votes, such as soldiers serving in Kosovo, and that may take weeks to finalise.

Al Gore has threatened to fight through the courts but his party has urged him to concede defeat to George W. Bush for the sake of America. I hope this will not be a bad omen for the new term under the Republicans. We shall see.

On 13th November, confirmation has now come through, by fax, that Marie's flights are booked and she has arranged to stay at the Dorchester Hotel, Park Lane, London W1, in her professional name, for the whole of December.

I have this picture of Marie in my mind, eight years old, and yet at this moment, it seems to me as if time stood still from the moment she left. Now, I shall see her again and to have Marie here with my grown-up family will be a conscious dream. It is almost too much to absorb that she is so interested to come across the world, on a memory. Perhaps my letters have rekindled the happiness of those days, or the need for the mutual interest and excitement we derived from everything around us. I pray that I can continue where we left off and that I don't regret opening up a memory which was laid to rest all those years ago.

Turning to nature and the beauty all around us, the next rush of wind will change the scene to barren winter with the last remaining golden leaves falling from the trees, but the sun has given us all a welcome boost for Monday morning; Kate stayed to avoid the recent flooding and we all enjoyed a musical Sunday evening.

I will just write a reminder that the Dome was the centre of a drama last week. A plot was uncovered months ago; thieves were planning to steal the De Beer diamonds which were on show in the Dome in the money zone. The magnificent Flying Squad were waiting, disguised as cleaners, with guns in bin bags and as the thieves arrived by literally driving through the side of the Dome, the criminals were arrested. Their plan was to steal the diamonds worth something in the region of £350 million and get away in a power boat along the Thames, in James Bond style. Well done, Intelligence.

15th November 2000

My dear Marie,

I have received your fax, detailing your flights and hotel booking; your choice of the Dorchester Hotel will be very appropriate for your needs. You will have easy access to the artistic venues in London and the hotel will be ideal to promote your work.

Kate and I leased a flat in Petty France, Victoria, from a Member of Parliament for a year in the early nineties. At that time Kate thought she might work in London and we felt it would be useful to improve our knowledge of the capital.

Before Michael and I were married, I commuted to London for 12 years and I feel completely at ease and in my natural environment in the West End. I love the sophistication, the buzz, the affluence and I am sure, from what I remember, that you will feel the same, particularly as you live in Sydney. Sadly, life is not quite the same now as it was in the sixties and one has to be vigilant and streetwise.

I have secured four tickets for a London show (to be a surprise) for the evening of 9th December. Michael and Jules will accompany us and we will drive to London.

Please fax, e-mail or telephone if you are worried or concerned about anything connected with the trip. We will be your 'base'; think of this as home throughout your stay.

We are envisaging postal difficulties here for the festive season, which have already begun with consistently late arrivals of the morning mail. This is due to a number of factors, including staff shortages, but I am not sufficiently au fait with the situation to talk about it.

Our gardener has just arrived to clear the covering of leaves from the lawns, so I will finish here and let's see what happens tomorrow.

Good wishes,

Jayne

114

From Jayne's diary

Marie will be arriving in two weeks, so I shall not take up her time by writing again. It has occurred to me that she may have been in touch with her brothers. I know of two brothers and she did speak of an older sister, but I am not sure of their whereabouts. I have no doubt she will visit them during her stay and I may receive a phone call from one of her brothers (or sister) anytime now to make contact.

There is a covering of frost this morning – the first of the season; the flooding is receding, but the new hazard is ice.

Preparations are under way for Marie's visit. New curtains, bedcover, linen and room sprays have brought the guest room to life if she wishes to stay; I have added some finishing touches such as a personal tray with tea and coffee facilities, crystal tumblers, a wineglass and a variety of refreshments in case of a sleepless night. She also has a TV, radio and magazines. Any other needs can soon be provided as we live so close to the town. We have the Internet and fax for communications as, of course, by staying at the Dorchester for most of her time, she will have standards in keeping with the rich and famous.

It is all so exciting!

Whilst waiting patiently for Marie's arrival, I have been thinking about the stamp album which she gave me just before she left this country. It became one of those precious childhood possessions which has grown in value over the years and I am now reassured that I was correct in keeping it away from the family library.

I remember Marie coming into school, in an agitated state, saying that the family had been given the news of her move and she wanted me to have the album, which was overfilled with stamps from all over the world. My father had given me an album when he knew of our interest and he even took the trouble to fill in my name and address, possibly realising the value that can be created with such a collection. Marie's album was so varied and interesting; the stamps were colourful and each one showed a picture or design appropriate to the country with the name given in the native language. If there was a stamp we had not seen before, we would use the *Stanley Gibbons Guide* to trace its origin.

When Marie gave me the album, it was almost in a way that she was giving it to me for safe-keeping and that it wasn't forever. At that point I wasn't sure about anything, but I was certain that the album needed great care and although the pages have now turned a creamy yellow, it is perfectly intact, together with my own collection, which has expanded over the years.

I shall find an appropriate time during her visit, when we are alone, to bring out the album and I am longing to see her reaction. It will be her decision, of course, as to what she wants to do with it.

Back to the present day – now that all the arrangements have been made for the coming month, I have decided to go to Cartier's in London to buy a present for Marie. I shall be looking for an emerald and diamond brooch to make a dazzling contrast to her auburn hair. It will be a small present, in size, so that taking it back to Australia will not be a problem. It will be a measure of our appreciation that she is making the effort to see us, apart from the amount of money she will incur on her trip. Next Tuesday, will be an ideal day before the daylight disappears altogether and the race for Christmas begins in earnest . . .

Friday 1st December was one of the most poignant, memorable and unbelievable days of my life. Michael and I drove

116

to Heathrow in good time to meet Marie's flight with Qantas. There was a one-hour delay at arrivals so we were able to prepare ourselves for the moment when she would appear through customs. Waiting is an ordeal for me at any time but the anticipation of seeing someone for the first time since the early post-war years was almost too much to bear and I had to exercise mind over matter and keep calm.

As Marie came through arrivals, I was not too sure at first and hesitated before I could be certain that the person was in fact Marie; but then I recognised an expression from the photos which she had sent to me. I caught her arm and a spontaneous smile flashed across her face as she realised that this was it – the meeting we had both been waiting for. She was just as I remember her, with the same auburn curls but with traces of silver highlights.

'Jayne – how lovely to see you,' she drawled with a slight Australian accent. As if neither of us could believe what was happening, we just stood and looked at one another as we used to in childish innocence and youthful inadequacy all those years ago.

Whilst experiencing momentary flashbacks, I tried to find some common ground, but automatic thoughts took over and I introduced her to Michael, who was standing back. He asked her how she felt after the long flight. She said, 'All right, at the moment, and I am thrilled to be back in England.' We all stood for a few more moments, totally unaware of everyone around us, as one does, gazing at one another and commenting on how we all looked, concluding that although many years had elapsed, we were still the same people and the passage of time had been kind.

Collecting our thoughts on what had to be done, we left for the journey to her hotel, settled her in for the remainder of the day to rest and prepare for our celebration tomorrow. Just before we left, she opened her hand luggage and brought out presents for the whole family, carefully wrapped with their names on each package. This was characteristic of Marie as I remember her. It was almost too much to absorb in one day; we then left and promised to phone her before nightfall.

I felt drained with emotion when I reached home but after a meal and some relaxation, I spoke to Marie about 8.30 to make arrangements and give her directions to our house when she would be the guest of honour at the dinner party on Saturday evening. She explained that after a good night's rest, she had arrangements to make relating to her work as an artist but she was looking forward to seeing us on Saturday evening . . .

The dinner party was an interesting occasion. Marie arrived at 7.45 by taxi, followed by our friends Andrew and Vanessa and Charles and Ailsa. Kate was here in the afternoon, helping with last minute preparations including setting up the candles and an oil burner which pleasantly perfumed the room without being too overpowering. Jules was coming and going at intervals and Peter was willing to help where necessary.

The expected number of guests was ten, so I had decided to give the catering to a well-respected firm in the area and they arrived at 7 p.m. with two appropriately dressed waitresses. On this occasion I needed to entertain, not work, and I was glad of the extra help.

Marie seemed to enjoy the choice of Ardennes pâté or salmon and asparagus with salad and wedges of brown bread. We followed with traditional English roast turkey, potatoes and a variety of vegetables and sauces with gravy. Desserts of fresh fruit salad and pavlova with optional cream were much appreciated. This was accompanied by a champagne toast to Marie, and with white and red wine. I, personally, supervised the after-dinner coffee and the

118

atmosphere was sumptuous with background music by Jules. I couldn't help thinking how appropriate it was when he selected the music 'Love Will Find a Way'.

Charles works for a Government body; he is academic, hypersensitive and has a good sense of humour. Ailsa, his wife, is a retired teacher, gentle, reserved but quietly good fun. Andrew manages his own companies – in fact, he will start up a company with any commercial potential. His personality is his fortune with a large, round smiling face and a loud voice which gets louder as the evening progresses and the wine flows – a lovable character. His wife Vanessa is his partner in business and it is quite noticeable in company that she tries to gain superiority over him in every way. He laughs at it and seems to love her all the more for the challenge.

As a group of people we gelled, putting the world right in our opinions, and Marie seemed very happy although a little tired from the jet lag towards the end of the evening. She brought a collection of photographs of her daughters Michaela, Olivia and their children, her late husband and various projects which she had designed over the years. Jules played a selection of late-night music and Aussie folk songs.

Marie stayed overnight in the specially prepared guest room and we said farewell to the other guests at about 1 a.m.

On Monday morning, I felt rejuvenated. The dinner party was a huge success, beyond our expectations; this is always partly to do with the input of the guests, and ours were marvellous.

Thinking back to Sunday morning, Michael, Marie and I were up and about by 9 a.m. and although a little tired, particularly Marie, we were very happy, still quite inebriated and ready to laugh at anything. After breakfast, we languished in the conservatory, hardly taking our eyes off Marie, and the conversation just flowed. One could not believe there had been a gap of over 50 years. She said that her family had to work very hard for an average income, in 1947, as in fact, we did here at that time. The temperatures, rising to 109 F in the shade made them ill and the homesickness was cruel, but she had her artistic talent and interest in life around her, which she clung to in those early years.

We then had a long discussion about the world in general and the changes since we were children. We felt the brutality and suffering in some areas had gone back to the dark ages and, again, Kosovo was our focal point. The Middle East and Ireland are still unresolved regions in the pursuit of a peaceful life. There were endless subjects to test our opinions, such as violence, crime and attacks on women, social attitudes today and one-parent families; as well as the lack of religious conviction and reliance on drugs. However, we also agreed that in many ways, life had improved since we were at school – conditions and labour-saving devices had given women a better life nowadays and equality for women had freed from domesticity those who wanted changes. Men and women were more 'as one' today and the divide between them had narrowed.

After several cups of coffee, I thought this might be the most appropriate time to bring out the stamp album. Marie had, in fact, forgotten it, but within a minute or two, the memory came flooding back and she spent several minutes 'lost' in the album. When she regained her composure, she started to pick out the various regions, explaining where the stamps came from – something I had never known. By late morning, the tiredness was overwhelming us and Marie said she should start to make her way to London to the hotel, where she would telephone Michaela and Olivia to let them know all was well. As she left, she said she would like me to keep the album as it had brought us together and it would be a reminder of our childhood for the rest of our lives. I will *never* forget that little girl with the auburn ringlets.

I met Marie at Harrods on Monday. We browsed for nearly an hour and she bought some small leather goods for Michaela and Olivia, her brother Roderick, his wife and two sons. She will be staying in Richmond with her brother for the weekend before Christmas.

We were then beginning to wilt, so we made our way to the restaurant for lunch. Marie explained that whilst she is in England, she needs to visit some of the arts centres and clients in the capital. Her commissions have spread to several capitals of the world and it would be beneficial to meet the people in person. She has two meetings arranged at the Dorchester and another at the client's office in Grosvenor Square. This will keep her busy until the week-end when Michael, Jules and I are taking her to the theatre.

Marie seems radiantly happy with all that is happening and described the Dorchester Hotel like a scene from a filmset, where she has already met some interesting people.

She went on to say that she would visit the Tate Gallery in its various forms and we talked about what we thought of the Tate Modern. Neither of us felt we had learned to appreciate modern art and that is probably our problem. I went on to say that I feel one has to like what one sees and appreciate the brilliance of the artist's portrayal of the subject. Unless this is present, then, I must confess, I have missed something.

We made our farewells with the arrangement that we would speak on the telephone and meet her on Saturday for the theatre trip . . .

*

Thursday 7th December. It is mild, which is lovely but perverse. It is certain that flu and colds will be spreading in these warm conditions. However, it is bright and dry, the trees are bare and travelling is easy, which helps so much at this busy time of the year.

It is taking a long time for me to settle down this morning. There seem to be so many balls in the air at the moment that it is hard to know which one to catch first. Marie is getting on with the business side of her trip until the weekend. I have been wrapping parcels and writing Christmas cards. Due to postal difficulties, I started early this year but I am writing them, with all the seasonal messages, in groups of six. In this way, there is time for other pressing work to be covered and the writing does not become too tedious.

I am just making a note of the news which has come through this week that euthanasia has been legalised in the Netherlands. This has been a contentious issue for many years and I hope that it will be practised with at least two or three people in agreement on the decision.

Marie will be interested that New South Wales is flooded. Heavy rainfall and flooding have been serious issues this year in various parts of the world and clearly, we need greater protection in the future.

The sun is now shining brilliantly, which has provided light during these otherwise dark days. The scene has changed from gales and heavy rain which tore across this part of the world again last night, but we have been spared the terror of falling trees.

Christmas decorations are cheerfully reminding us that it is the season of goodwill but controlled panic is the overall mood today – there is a lot happening and more will be happening. Our Christmas card list is now finished and the parcels to Esther and Aunt Bethany are on their way. There is much to do with the way that the festive season has grown but at the same time, so many people are suffering with stress that panic has to be avoided.

Michael, Jules and I will be travelling to London tomorrow to take Marie to the theatre so, on a daily basis, we are feeling fairly relaxed and happy that all is well at the moment.

Kate, Jules and Peter are committed to work, parties and visiting friends, and spiritual optimism is in the air . . .

Michael and I stayed in London on Saturday night after the theatre, which I would describe as a sumptuous evening. We travelled back yesterday when everywhere seemed to be deserted except the shopping areas. The scenery was grey and bare but we felt an inner warmth and radiance from the high life in London. *The King and I* with Elaine Page took us to a different part of the world with its eastern flavour, and although it has been portrayed by many people throughout the years, every new cast brings something special to the show. If one enjoys the theatre and London life, it is such a boost for the spiritually low and I recommend it. My view is, as one finishes, book tickets for the next one in two months' time. I am still slightly numb from the weekend but that should improve after lunch today.

I have noticed how Marie takes everything in her stride and how the child I knew has developed into a capable, dynamic person able to negotiate with the chairman of the board and yet homely and down to earth on family matters. It is all there in childhood, just waiting to grow and develop, with the right encouragement and opportunity.

During the coming week last-minute business and Christmas preparations will be taking place before the long break into the New Year. Marie and I will be in touch by phone but I shall not see her again until next Wednesday, when we will be making a pilgrimage to our infants' school.

She has various business meetings planned for this week and a social evening at the Dorchester on Saturday, so I must now come down to earth and attend to the work of the day; Michael has already been in the office for two hours.

Marie and I have spoken on the phone several times since we saw her in London and her trip seems to have been beneficial on the business side. She is finding it a new and rewarding challenge, although she admits the changes in technology are certainly an improvement but in some ways a hindrance and it is easier at times just to pick up the telephone. I agree that the computer has changed and advanced so quickly that there are bound to be shortfalls. She spent a very pleasant evening with some visitors to the Dorchester Hotel on Saturday last, while Michael and I went to a Christmas party in our village.

Thursday 21st December – Yesterday Marie and I went back to Chetworth School. I collected her from the station at 11 a.m. and we drove to the school where we were infants. I felt uneasy, at one point, as to whether this was the right decision. Until now it had seemed a good idea to retrace our early years together but I started to wonder whether the memories would be a positive experience for Marie or whether it might bring back the trauma of her early life.

As we approached the school gates I realised my fears were unfounded as she seemed to show excitement and interest. The school was closed for the Christmas holidays but there was a pathway which ran parallel to the frontage. Railings separated the school and playground from the pathway and we could clearly see that it was all very much the same as we remembered the layout in 1947.

In those post-war years, we would run, stop, swing on the railings, brush down our hands, pick up our belongings and run again until we reached the gate at the far end of the school which was close to the infants' classroom. However, yesterday we were happy to sit for a minute or two on the conveniently placed benches along the pathway, whilst rapidly taking in any changes which had crept in over the years. Obviously the buildings looked older and extensions had been made but, to our relief, it had not fallen into neglect or been demolished and built over, as one might expect through the years.

We sat for a few minutes and retreated back into time. I turned to Marie with a smile and said, 'What can you remember?' She said, 'We started at 8.45; I can remember Miss Lamley taking the register.' We both agreed she was our favourite teacher. 'Then we walked in lines to the assembly hall across the playground. Each form lined up for hymns and prayers and there was an upright piano in the corner by the platform. "All Things Bright and Beautiful" was my favourite hymn and the whole school seemed to use their voices to show their love of the words and music. After assembly, we filed back to our classrooms and the day began. The desks had ink wells which the form monitor filled every morning, but we had to be seven or eight to use ink with thin wooden pens with nibs and blotting paper. Reading and arithmetic were compulsory every day.' Marie turned to me and said, 'Oh, yes and there were writing lessons two or three times each week with the Marion Richardson books. The education and learning were so good in those days Jayne, before TV and computers. Everything we did, whether it was reading, writing, arithmetic, drawing, painting, crafts or whatever was in the pursuit of learning.' We both agreed that we see the difference in the way children spend their time nowadays.

At this point I interrupted her and added, 'My earliest recollections were the Dan books and the A. & B. textbooks for maths, or was it B. & A.?'

'Good Lord.' She sat up and looked surprised. 'So we did; we worked through those every morning and I can vaguely remember daily Scripture lessons, geography, history – oh! and art, nature study and gardening with Miss Woodley – the poor lady had very hard hands from blackboard chalk and gardening.' We giggled and I remarked that it was the poor *pupil* when she slapped their legs.

I reminded Marie of the annual intelligence tests and how we were not told the results or what they were leading to, which is what I wanted to know at that time; the regular spelling tests following long lists of spellings which we had to take home and, of course, music, physical training – PT – as it was called in those days – and needlework. Form monitors collected crates of milk with straws for every child, unless they had a note. If the school bell rang Vivienne George and I took it in turns to run errands for the Headmistress, Miss Cooke.

'Marie, do you remember the bottle of coloured sand from the Isle of Wight, which I dropped in the playground? I felt as if the whole school was looking at me, but of course they were too busy with their own interests. I could not believe my bad luck, but it taught me from that moment to be especially careful with anything precious or important, particularly relationships.'

The memories were flooding in now and although we were older I realised we were exactly the same people, and to have regained the warmth, excitement and love of life which we felt as children was pure contentment. Although it was a chilly December day and we were dressed in winter coats sitting on a weather-beaten, slightly damp bench, we remembered our coded letters to each other, the gangs of boys who teased the girls – but bullying was unheard of and did not happen to us. Fingers on lips was the worst punishment for speaking and our group always met 'at the bush' for daily planning for lunch time and after school.

The winters were long, from October to June, with snow lying about for weeks; fogs were so thick that buses did not run and you could not see a pace in front of you. We made toast over fires on toasting forks, listening to 'Uncle Mac' on BBC radio at 5 p.m. Horse meat was on sale for dogs but unfit for human consumption and the American soldiers were here. Food parcels were arriving with packets of sweets for school children – spinning tops, kerb stones, hopscotch and skipping ropes were our tools of friendship. I reminded Marie of the importance of the first ring binder which Vivienne George brought into school. Somehow she always managed to be first with everything. Juggling with two balls was a much practised skill and tap dancing on quarry tiles brought a buzz to the kitchens at tea time.

Horse-drawn 'rag and bone' carts were still trundling the streets and large portraits of Winston Churchill, our war-time leader, could be seen in windows and doorways with the Union Jack.

The polio disease was very frightening and instead of swimming at the local baths, we joined the Red Cross Society, who were vigorously recruiting after the war.

Marie again reminded me of the needlework cases which Vivenne George and I were given for achieving top and second places in class, which became embarrassing. It seemed automatic that we became prefects and were asked to run errands for the Headmistress but this seemed to change after I had a head-on collision with her one day when running at high speed past her room.

'After you left for Australia, Marie, Vivienne and I were heavily into gymkhanas but we went to different grammar schools at eleven and I went to music college in London for three years. I always thought at the time that we would be friends for life but, sadly, we all travel in different directions; I have always found that hard to accept.

'I wonder what we would have said if we had been asked "What do you think will be happening in the year 2000?" We might have said, "We will probably be dead" when considering such a distant milestone in our lives; or we might have said "We will be travelling in space rockets". It is interesting to see how science in all aspects, including medicine has advanced, and electronics, aviation, technology and design have rocketed in progress. Do you find yourself looking forward or backwards?'

Marie thought for a moment and then, still deep in thought, replied, 'I enjoy memories of the past, but positively look to the future.'

Our reminiscing turned to after-school hours, when we walked home at 3.30 (it felt safe in those days). We bought drinks for pennies en route and at home we would switch on the radio for *Children's Hour*. Monty, a dog, and Peckham, a cat, talked to one another over the radio about what was happening in their day. Our interests were books, stamps, knitting, dolls, bicycles, games and walking on stilts in the garden.

After a while, Marie turned to me and said, 'You know, Jayne, I always thought that you and Vivienne George were the brightest, sincerest and most sensible girls in our year.' I flushed, for whatever reason, but I knew there was a real friendship between Marie and me.

I retaliated by saying, 'Did you ever think you would be here again, Marie?'

She thought for a moment and then replied, 'I always felt I would come home one day, especially as my brothers are here, but unless you had written to me and taken me back in time to those wonderful, carefree days, I might not have made the effort; it is like a pleasing dream and such a deep experience to relive memories which I had to forget.'

I went on to recall that we rounded off our time at Chetworth and then prepared with everything new, even pencil cases, to present ourselves for registration at the senior school. I was open-minded about it and had no idea of the challenge which was ahead. This started from day one, in the first form, and the level was entirely different from junior school, bearing in mind there were girls there who went on to be doctors, teachers and lawyers, and many obtained scholarships to university. The first form, on reflection, is always a testing time and more or less determines one's level right through the school. Unknowingly at the time, I steered a middle course, believing that it was 'not done' to work very hard and shine above others, if that were possible. It would probably not be popular and it would be too competitive for me. However, I completed my schooling at 17 with respectable O level passes in GCE and knew exactly what I wanted to do – that was to go out in the big wide world of business, preferably in the West End of London. I spent a further year studying for the necessary qualifications and my dream was fulfilled at 19 when I started working in a London exporting business. From then on, it seemed important to gain as much experience as possible in different businesses to make life more interesting. Seven years later I met Michael and we were married. Kate, Jules and Peter arrived and their schooling became another exciting interest for me as well.

I turned to Marie and said, 'I think I am now catching up with when I first started writing to you. The children's formal education is more or less finished but Peter continues taking certificates in whatever interests him.'

It was getting cold, so we walked back to the car. Before we left the area, we looked at Marie's house nearby from which she emigrated in 1947. She remarked that it looked so tiny in comparison with her home today. Then we drove to the shops which had provided the drinks. They were still in business but the faces behind the counters seemed expressionless, compared with the 'father and mother' figures who knew us all those years ago.

Seeing a deserted Chetworth gave us a better landscape from which we could gather our memories. This was *our* school and it would have been a different Chetworth if we had seen it in progress today.

Friday 22nd December

This morning Roderick arrived at 11 a.m. to take Marie, who had stayed overnight, to Richmond. I was not at all surprised by Roderick. As I opened the door, I could see such a likeness with Marie that I felt at ease straight away, as if he were a brother of mine or a close relative. He had Marie's relaxed manner, spontaneous smile and greying, auburn hair. Although Roderick is taller, the family mould was apparent.

Marie was waiting at the lounge door and it was a pleasure to see their faces as they met. So many thoughts must have been going through their minds at that point – joy, nervousness, trepidation – after 20 years apart. After a few minutes, I left Marie and Roderick to talk between themselves while I made coffee. On returning to the lounge, the conversation turned to the family – how we were all distantly related and Roderick mentioned Malcolm, their other brother, who is a teacher living in Dorset. Roderick and Malcolm meet two or three times a year, in Poole, where Malcolm has a waterside home and motor yacht. We all agreed it was a great idea to encourage Marie back to England and Roderick added, 'Particularly as it was not our idea to move to Australia'. Marie had a more feminine outlook on the situation and could see that her father wanted to give them a better life. She went on to say that she felt at home in both Sydney and London. I thought this seemed to be fairly typical of the adaptable, subservient, female temperament, as opposed to the male, who tends to know what he wants and can be less accommodating.

After a couple of cups of refreshing coffee, Roderick checked the time. He stood up and with a warm and prolonged handshake, he thanked me in a most charming way for all that we had arranged. He hoped that Michael and I would visit his home in Richmond and meet his family sometime next year. I replied by saying we would be delighted to meet them and we made our way to the door. Just then, Marie asked if she could telephone Malcolm in Poole before she left. By the time I had cleared away the coffee, they were ready to leave and we made our farewells until Christmas Eve, when she will be returning to spend Christmas with us.

Dry, bright, sunny weather mixed with wet, windy, fog and frost have all come our way during the last week but the grounds have now been cleared of debris. There is a steady exodus of motorists for the Christmas break and family problems are minimal at present, in fact, there is more optimism amongst the young ones than I have known for a long time. As they are getting older, I can see they are coming to terms with what is on the agenda of life with the right attitude and necessary hard work. I am also pleased to see that they are getting their priorities right, in my estimation, as they reach the milestone of 30 years of age.

On the subject of worldly matters, I just want to make a note that George W. Bush has now been elected the President of America after weeks of legal arguments through the courts. Certain ballot boxes had not been counted and there were thousands of American absentee votes abroad in places such as Kosovo, where American soldiers are stationed, which were presumably omitted from the count.

131

However, the final court ruling stated that no further counting would be allowed.

In this country, we have received the news that Murray Walker our popular Formula 1 commentator, will be retiring at the age of 77 next year after the 2001 season. Motor racing will never be quite the same for me but nothing lasts forever.

Having said family problems are minimal, fate nearly struck a blow for us this week. Jules went to London with his firm for a Christmas party. They were planning to have a meal, a river trip and then view London from the London Eye. He left in the morning, but during the afternoon, news was coming through on the radio that the London Eye had been taken over by Turkish extremists who were possibly holding hostages, to publicise their cause on human rights in Turkey . . . At this point, Jules could have been a hostage. However, later on it became clearer that the extremists were demonstrating at lunchtime, which was possibly an hour before the office party was due to arrive. It was a shock but Jules arrived home safely in the early evening, explaining that he had narrowly missed the incident. Each and every one of us must have a guardian angel.

Last night I was unable to relax. Thoughts bombarded my mind like missiles, speeding in all directions; this was all to do with last-minute preparations before everything closes down for the holiday. I tried to clear my mind and relax but I knew that I would not be able to sleep so I had to turn to my natural remedy of putting my thoughts on paper. I produced something like an Advent plan for the remaining days before Christmas. Whether the boys had Christmas presents for Kate and on which day the refuse would be collected were, ironically, the subject of my anguish. Is this efficiency beyond what is healthy? However, it worked like magic and I only remember awaking at dawn.

I am now working to my plan as Marie will return on

Sunday 24th and it is important to work but not get overtired. Peter has been helpful while Kate and Jules are finishing their last-minute shopping . . .

When Marie and Kate arrived on Christmas Eve, I realised that nothing more could be done for the festive cause; it was some relief to know that the preparations would come to an end; the stage was set, and any omissions would be accepted or laughed at; we just had to enjoy ourselves. However, there was still work to do and this had to be done whilst being available at the same time for conversation. I was able to prepare and cook the sage and onion turkey stuffing and make the Yorkshire puddings to accompany the turkey on Christmas Day. Charred Yorkshire puddings were very nearly the result of playing a few carols on the organ, but I managed to salvage them, giving myself the worst.

Michael and Kate left home about 10 o'clock to drive to London for the Midnight Mass at Westminster Cathedral and by the time the sherry trifle was prepared and the salad chopped and washed, I was physically drained. This is something I try to avoid on the day before any auspicious occasion but sometimes it cannot be avoided. Marie and I decided to retire to our beds about 11 p.m. and the house eventually quietened down after Michael and Kate returned about 2 a.m.

On Christmas morning, sacks of presents are delivered to each bedroom door in the house – doors begin to open and someone dashes out to make a delivery and tiptoes back; then another door opens, until with relief, every mission is complete. This began over 30 years ago and the children have now joined in the fun. We open our bags of surprises and although a little tired, there is always a feeling of joy that this is the celebration of the birth of Jesus and we can now enjoy the results of our efforts throughout December.

By the time Marie appeared, smiling as always, the turkey was cooking and we were ready to leave for the family service at church. We were unable to park, so there was a fair walk up a steep gradient in driving wind and rain. When we reached the church, it was full, with people standing, and very noisy with coughing and sneezing; a legacy of the mild winter. There had obviously been an epidemic of colds and flu in the neighbouring village which hadn't reached us.

After a memorable lunch, with Marie completing our table of six, we watched the Queen with her moving Christmas message and TV broadcast, opened our tree presents and relaxed, giving much attention to Marie. I am very pleased with Kate, Jules and Peter in the way they have welcomed my school friend into the family. Rejection by any one of the family would have caused such emotional conflict at probably the most difficult time of the year. We had plans for playing bridge or other games, but everyone wanted to relax after the feasting.

Boxing Day, in years gone by, was spent with Michael's parents. Another Christmas meal and games filled the day. But since both grandparents died, we book tickets for the theatre or dinner at a local restaurant. This year, particularly as Marie is with us, I booked tickets to see the Russian ice stars perform *Phantom of the Opera*.

After a leisurely morning and a light lunch, we left home at 2.30 p.m. and drove through deserted streets to a neighbouring town. The town buildings always create an inward buzz for me and when we arrived the theatre was filling with smiling, happy people. There was a warm and inviting atmosphere inside the building, which is divided into four areas of entertainment. Having climbed the stairs to the large concert hall, we secured a programme and found our seats in good time to savour the excitement of the curtain being raised.

The fitness and brilliance of the artistes was breathtaking. The ballet on ice, spectacular rope-work from the roof of the building and, for an added third dimension, swinging on the ropes by the artistes *into* the audience, made us all part of one big show. Marie was 'lost' in the performance, which, I must confess, is how I like to feel at the theatre.

Most restaurants were closed after the show, so I put together a pasta meal at home which spontaneously concluded an interesting and restful day.

On 27th December, a Wednesday, and the day after the ice show, we felt energetic and had a sense of relief that Christmas had been a success. Our reaction to skating here is always the same – we want to find the nearest ice rink and re-enact what we have seen – but we all agreed we had been out and about enough for the time being and it would be pleasant to spend a quiet day going through old photographs, some of which go back to the days of Chetworth. Michael also has photos from childhood, so, knowing Marie as I do, I knew she would be engrossed in the pictorial account of our by-gone years.

After breakfast, I brought out the many albums we have compiled since 1968, as well as books which covered the forties and fifties. We started at the beginning and Marie recognised the garden where I grew up with Esther. We spent more time in the garden than indoors and the memories came rushing in again. By lunch time, we had covered up to 1982, when Michael, the children and I moved to our country estate.

Marie was fascinated by the dozens of photos of that era. She recalled all that was happening with Ralph and the girls in Sydney at that time and the hours just disappeared. We were unable to finish before dinner as we talked for hours, but we cooked a meal for the family, in the hope that we would be able to return to the albums, but I somehow had my doubts. A sore throat was beginning to indicate that I had not escaped the flu germs on Christmas Day.

As the coffee was brewing on Thursday morning, Marie came into the kitchen and from her smile and bright eyes, I knew she had some ideas which she was about to impart. I felt equally enthusiastic for anything she might suggest as reassurance of her pleasure during her stay. My family were busy with their own daily routine and Marie started to tell me about some delicious Australian recipes she had gathered over the years and wondered whether I would like her to cook today. I just had a feeling that she may be a tiny bit homesick and I readily agreed to whatever she would like to concoct.

I have a full selection of herbs and spices and the menu she suggested was made up from large prawns, mushrooms, courgettes and red peppers, spiced and grilled, served on egg pasta with green salad, but she explained the key to the flavour was locked in the spice. Chocolate mousse with rum and raisins would follows.

In spite of a covering of snow and ice, we drove to the village to buy some fresh ingredients and Marie prepared the feast for the evening. I offered any help where necessary and the dishwasher was indispensable, as always. By the early afternoon, we had an array of food with which the family was fascinated.

I am, again, very impressed with the way Michael, Kate, Jules and Peter have reacted to Marie – they showed immense appreciation of the food, which was so important to me at this late stage of her visit, and I think it is fairly remarkable that all the temperaments have been compatible. It would be so sad if there had been a clash of personalities, which is so often unavoidable, and Marie had returned to Australia with our friendship threatened by events. I hope it would surmount any outside influence but, perhaps, that is too idealistic to take for granted. However, all is well and the happiness I am always trying to achieve is alive and flourishing; how lovely.

Marie promised to send some recipes, which, apart from the culinary delights, told me that our friendship was intact.

29th December (Friday) – I have now developed a sore and aching throat but I shall keep going and, hopefully, it will not deteriorate into flu. There are only a few days left now before Marie returns to Australia. I have asked her whether she would sketch some pictures for me, which I will frame. She said she would love to sketch and would be happy to spend all day producing whatever I have in mind. As I still have a case of artist's materials from my graduation as a designer, it was not difficult to sort out what was needed and, in fact, we had quite a lot of fun going through all the pens, pencils, felt tips, crayons and charcoal which, it seemed, had ever been invented . . . Conveniently, I also had a large pad of cartridge paper which was perfect for the sketching.

Marie thought our dining room would be an ideal room in which to spread out during the daytime and she set about her task in an organised and inspired mood. As our earliest memories were all to do with horses, that was the first subject. It was a joy which sent shivers through me when I saw her outline a prancing stallion with the ease that I would draw up my daily plan. She took about an hour to put the finishing touches and the sketch was the epitome of beauty, vigour, strength and the love of freedom. It would bring life to any room and I adored the finished product. She was equally pleased and looked flushed and radiant when the work was complete.

She said she would do two sketches. If I agreed, the second one would be a collection of small animal sketches to include koala bears, wallabies, kangaroos and crocodiles in the water to create an Australian landscape. I thought it was a brilliant idea and I left her to get on with it as I had work to do. When she had finished, I was really lost for words – her talent was amazing. She said she had drawn similar sketches for an advertising firm in Sydney, but she had made one or two changes to the drawings to create new originals. The lines, the shading, the understanding of the muscle and bone structures brought the creatures to life, which reinforced my view that I appreciate representational art, whether traditional or modern, and Marie has a very rare gift.

On Saturday 30th December, Michael and the boys were busy with their own plans – Kate had returned to her flat – so Marie and I decided to have our hair styled for the New Year celebrations. We booked appointments for the afternoon and left about lunch time to browse in the shops and have a coffee and a sandwich for, probably, the last time together. We toured a branch of Dickins & Jones, which was a dazzling experience, and then went on to meet our stylists.

Relaxing in the luxurious and sophisticated salon, Marie asked for a simple style, swept back with curls, and I settled for my shoulder-length pageboy. It was very therapeutic and we felt it had been another day well-spent at this quiet time of year.

After the evening meal, I played a selection of music on the organ for an hour or so and Marie remarked that my music training must have happened after she left England. I explained that auditions took place at Chetworth in 1950; after the initial test, maybe three or four pupils went to Trinity College in London to sing and play an instrument and I believe two were awarded Junior Exhibitions for three years, of which I was a lucky one; but we were a musical family, so it seemed to follow. Marie seemed fascinated to recall that era once again . . .

I have found some time to write about what is happening while Marie is in her room preparing for the evening.

It is 5 p.m. on New Year's Eve, Peter's birthday and the first anniversary of the Millennium. We went for a short walk this morning to get some air, although there are still patches of black ice. Gale-force winds are now lashing the trees and driving rain is beating against the windows. If this turns to ice tonight when the temperature drops, the roads will become ice rinks and we may have to consider staying at the hotel where we have booked dinner. Michael will probably say it will be all right to drive home and heaven knows what may happen. I am feeling really worried.

For several years since becoming aware of global warming, we have not had to think about the weather when making arrangements for New Year's Eve, although it was always a subject of discussion 30 years ago.

Peter's birthday has taken my mind away from tonight's celebrations. We all went to the dining room at 4 p.m. to have tea and birthday cake and give him his presents, while we crooned 'Happy Birthday'. This made a pleasant interlude to an otherwise quiet but reasonably stressful day.

1.1.01 – Thank God – and I really mean that. Although the winds and rain continued all night, we avoided the icy, country roads and we returned home about 1.30 a.m. safe and sound. We are tired but bubbly today and my relief is immense that all went well.

Peter danced with Marie and I was proud of my young gentleman, who had made an effort to look immaculately dressed.

Relaxation is all that we can think of now and apart from providing some snacks and dinner tonight, that is all we shall be doing today. The winding down is so welcome after weeks of pressure and just the basic work will be covered for the next few days.

Marie was busy in her room until lunch time. During the afternoon she asked me if she could make a call to her daughters, confirming her arrival at the weekend. I said, 'Of course; I shall be in the lounge for a while.'

When she came into the lounge, she sat down and seemed to be deep in thought. She had spoken to Michaela, her elder daughter, who said she would meet her at the airport on her return. To my surprise, Marie, who until now had been very composed and, seemingly, in control of her life, began to explain that Michaela and Olivia were both very much like Ralph. They all excelled at sport, which, of course, is encouraged in Australia. He coached them at an early age in swimming and badminton and they spent many hours together in training until, as teenagers, they had become soulmates. They were devasted by his death and although there was a bond between Marie and her daughters, she never quite felt it was the same as the spiritual love they had for Ralph.

Momentarily, I was a little lost for words, but deeply interested in the situation, and I sat for a few minutes thinking through what Marie had said. This sudden baring of the soul made me wonder whether Marie was having doubts about going back to Australia.

Again, childhood memories could be playing a large part in how she was feeling – being dragged away from all that she loved to make a new life, and having returned years later, only to have to go back again. Suddenly, I felt a slight inward panic that I had been responsible for this. I said a few words to the effect that Michaela and Olivia probably loved and admired her in a different way from Ralph – she was brilliantly talented, successful and she was their mother who was there, when they came home from training. 'You are probably appreciated far more than you will ever realise, but of course, I have never met the girls.' But I was not in a position to say any more.

Marie's expression showed that she was inwardly disturbed and I asked her to help me to prepare dinner, to save her from sinking deeper into the trauma which she had experienced in 1947 when she left England.

After a few minutes, I realised that she was mature enough to deal with the situation, as I think I would be nowadays, and after the evening meal, the subject was forgotten.

The following day, after a restless night, I waited to see how Marie was feeling before taking any positive view of how I should react to her 'cry for help' yesterday. It was only natural for her to have mixed feelings and apprehension; she had a long flight ahead of her, after an unusual reunion, and she was probably anticipating the readjustment, again, on her return to Australia.

She was calm and smiling as she came into the kitchen and I knew she had come to terms with what was ahead of her. There are many positive aspects for her to look forward to and, most of all, the trip had been worthwhile.

About 10 a.m. Marie asked if she could order a taxi, as she should really return to London today to finish off some business, do some packing and say goodbye to people she had met at the hotel. Michael agreed to drive me to the Dorchester on Friday, where we would meet Marie and take her to Heathrow for her return flight to Sydney.

Marie had left by lunch time and I must confess I was feeling a little below par with the lack of sleep, the aftermath of a cold and general emotional upheaval. I was contented, however, that Marie had become just the sort of person I had expected her to be from my early memories.

The day was bright, dry and sunny and our gardener was working so I had to quickly turn my mind to my involvements for the next two days. As I spoke to Michael, Kate, Jules and Peter, I thanked them for all their kindness and understanding in having Marie with us. They are interested in Marie and said they had enjoyed her visit . . .

On Friday 5th January 2001, Michael and I left home about 9.30 a.m. for the drive to London. It was a pleasant journey and we arrived at the Dorchester at 10.45. Marie was ready, her luggage packed and she ordered coffee for us before making the trip to Heathrow. In the meantime, her account was settled and I must say she was looking the epitome of a successful, dynamic globe-trotter. Her grooming and attention to detail was an inspiration and I felt full of admiration for Marie, who had excelled in spite of adversity in her youth.

We left the hotel about midday and Michael drove to Heathrow. He is familiar with the airport, having made many trips over the years, and the arrival was reasonably trouble-free. We had some time to spare, so we resigned ourselves to the fact that this would be another leisurely day well spent.

As the time was drawing near for her departure, Marie, in a relaxed but positive way, said how much she had enjoyed this trip. She said she would keep writing and I would probably hear from her within a few days. She then said, 'Please keep writing back, Jayne', and that was just what I wanted to hear. It was so important to me as well.

After her departure, Michael and I left the airport to begin the journey home. I felt a sadness and yet a sense of relief that everything had been so worthwhile. Marie, the child who had shone in the crowd, had become a free spirit now, programmed by that early experience in 1947, but I knew the cherished memory from all those years ago would be with me for the rest of my life. I hope to see her again.

Dear Jayne,

I am now back in Sydney and I must admit I feel quite inebriated, not through alcohol, but just through the happiness of knowing what life has to offer if one can cope with hardship. I shall say to my granddaughters, when they are old enough, never give up however difficult situations may seem because invariably, with faith, your life will turn out right in the end.

Thank you so much Jayne. It was such a pleasure meeting you, Michael, Kate, Jules and Peter; how proud you must be of them. It was a wonderful idea when you decided to write to me and I shall be looking for your letters for as long as you feel you can write.

Your dear friend

Marie

THE END

Friendship

Caring and common ground are
the seeds of friendship it seems;
then trust, respect and forgiveness
follow later, in all that they mean.